THE
BILLIONAIRE'S
Secret Heart

THE
BILLIONAIRE'S
Secret Heart

IVY LAYNE

The Billionaire's Secret Heart

Copyright © 2016 by Ivy Layne

Edited by Valorie Clifton

Cover by Jacqueline Sweet

Paperback Design by Silver Heart Publishing

Find out more about the author and upcoming books online at www. ivylayne.com

Also by Ivy Layne

Don't Miss Out on New Releases, Free Stories
and More!!
Join Ivy's Readers Group!
Ivylayne.com/readers-group

The Billionaire's Secret - Novella Duology
The Billionaire's Secret Heart
The Billionaire's Secret Love

Scandals of the Bad Boy Billionaires
The Billionaire's Pet
The Billionaire's Promise

About

The Billionaire's Secret Heart

Josephine

It was the worst blind date in the history of the universe, until Holden Winters swept in and rescued me.

Are you kidding? Holden Winters?

A scion of the notorious Winters family, Holden is gorgeous, wealthy, and brilliant. He dates socialites and pop stars, not computer science grad students more comfortable in a hoodie than couture.

Our night together was a fantasy...and a huge mistake.

Holden

I don't usually steal other guy's dates. I don't have to. A look is all it takes, and the women fall over themselves to get to me. Then I saw Josephine, sitting with her dweeb of a date, just waiting for a man who could appreciate her lush curves and sharp brain.

When she ghosted on me, I shouldn't have been so shocked, but women never walk away from me. Josephine thought she could call the shots—she didn't realize that a Winters man always gets what he wants. And I wanted her.

CONTENTS

CHAPTER ONE

JOSEPHINE

*I*T WAS OFFICIAL. I WAS ON THE WORST BLIND DATE IN the history of womankind. You can trust me when I say that. I'm a scientist, and I rarely exaggerate. It started when Stuart picked me up, his hair slicked back with enough product to lube every rusted bike chain in Atlanta. Did I mention that's what he was driving? A bike.

No, not a motorcycle. I've never ridden that kind of bike, but I might have been up for it with the right guy. Definitely not with Stuart, which wasn't a problem since he showed up on a ten-speed circa 1985. I never rode the handlebars of a bike when I was a kid. I was too busy with school. But at twenty-three, I wasn't looking to try it out—and definitely not on a date.

I ended up driving us to dinner. Not the most auspicious beginning, but I was willing to give Stuart the benefit of the doubt. I was a geek—a grad student at Georgia Tech in the Computer Sciences department—and I knew my share of socially awkward people who were pretty cool when you got to know them. I wasn't going to judge.

I really wasn't. I tried not to. He was good looking enough, if a little bland, but I wasn't a goddess myself, so I wouldn't write him off just because he wasn't gorgeous. Plus, he was my advisor's nephew, and she was fantastic, so I didn't want to ditch him and hurt her feelings. All my good intentions flew out the window right around the time he eyed my rounded figure and told the waitress we didn't need appetizers or any high-calorie drinks.

Excuse me? Like he was one to talk. Where I was blessed with more than abundant curves, he resembled a skeleton. Neither of us were going to win any hot body contests, and he wasn't in any position to comment on the way I looked.

I rolled my eyes, ordered a margarita, and sat back to watch the date slide into disaster. Two drinks later, I was completely zoned out as Stuart droned on about his dissertation.

A small part of me could sympathize. My specialization was Human-Computer Interaction, and if I wanted to watch someone's eyes glaze over, all I had to do was start talking about my current research project.

That's why *I* was polite enough not to talk about it—unlike my date, who seemed happy to go on and on about the effect of diversifying expenditures for political lobbyists. I'm not that well-versed in finance and economics, but I'm pretty sure Stuart was studying ways for lobbyists to influence the political system without being caught violating the laws of political donations. So he wasn't just rude and boring. He was also kind of evil.

Unfortunately, at that point, I was on my third margarita. While he looked over the check, he mentioned that he had a VIP invitation to Mana, the hottest club in town. I had no interest in Stuart, but I'd always wanted to go to Mana. It was nearly impossible to get in, especially for a girl who spent most of her time in jeans and a hoodie.

You needed to be hot to make it to the front of the line. You can imagine the type—tall, thin, gorgeous, perfectly dressed. Not me, on every count. The only other way into the club was to score one of the exclusive VIP invites, a small, round gold disc. I'd seen one once, and it had reminded me of the gold coins awarded to a gamer after vanquishing an enemy. Stuart pulled the coin from his pocket and waved it in the air, the golden gleam catching my eye. It looked like the real thing.

I didn't want to spend another second with Stuart. Just moments before, I'd been planning my escape, chalking up the evening to a waste of good makeup. Now I was tempted to stay. When was I going to get another chance to get into Mana?

"How did you get it?" I asked, suspicious. Stuart did not strike me as a guy with the connections to get a VIP invite to Mana.

"Someone owed me a favor," he said, trying to be mysterious.

After three margaritas and more than an hour of boredom, my manners were wearing thin, and I asked, "Is it real?" I'd heard about counterfeits rolling around town. I wanted to go to Mana, but I didn't want to be turned away from the door with a fake coin.

His eyes narrowed in annoyance, and Stuart said, "I got it from a senior I'm tutoring. He had some issues with a paper and I fixed them. He couldn't pay me, so he gave me this."

My tipsy brain skated around what kind of 'fixing' Stuart had done to score such a prize. Hmm, so he was boring, rude, and probably helping students cheat. Did I really want to spend more time with this guy just to get into a club that was probably going to be loud and crowded? Yes. Yes, I did.

VIP invites to Mana were notoriously hard to get, and if I didn't fit the mold of the typical Mana female, Stuart wouldn't exactly get past the velvet rope either. Did I mention he was wearing a corduroy blazer with elbow patches, a plaid shirt, and kakis? He looked like a stereotypical stuffy professor.

The CS department isn't known for our sartorial splendor, though. We lean more toward jeans and t-shirts with ironically geeky sayings under our hoodies. But even at our worst, we were a step above Stuart's lack of style. Not that I was dressed in my usual slacker wear. My roommate, Emily, another CS grad student, was one of the few exceptions to the typical geek's approach to fashion. She hadn't been on a date in over a year. I thought she was beautiful, but she was also cripplingly shy and obsessed with her research, resulting in a complete lack of a social life. But she had a killer wardrobe no one saw outside her lab and our apartment. We also wore the same size—my fabulously good luck. She'd spent over an hour dressing me, and the result was the best I'd looked in years. Maybe ever. If I went home, it would be a total waste, and Emily would be so disappointed. She'd been excited that at least one of us had a date.

"Let's go," I said, draping my wrap around my shoulders and picking up my purse. Stuart raised one finger to stop me and held up the bill the waitress had left.

"Your half is twenty-three, seventy-five."

"Does that include the tip?" I asked, not bothering to hide the sarcasm dripping from my voice. Stuart was oblivious. He gave me an owlish blink.

"Of course. An eight percent tip since the service was a little slow."

I shook my head and pulled a twenty and a ten from my purse. I wasn't rolling in cash. Actually, money was a little tight since my hours had been cut back this semester, but our waitress hadn't been slow. She'd been great. I'd waited tables during my undergrad, and I knew it wasn't an easy job. Tight budget or not, there was no way I was going to screw over our waitress.

Not trusting Stuart, I took the black pleather folder containing our bill and his cash from his hands, scanned it and added my contribution. Mana had better be the most amazing club in existence to justify spending any more time with this guy.

We hit the street outside the restaurant, and I started to walk in the direction of Mana. It was a good eight or ten blocks, but I'd had too much tequila to drive and I couldn't afford a ride. The walk wouldn't kill me, though in Emily's heels, my toes would be begging for mercy by the time we got there. Stuart complained about my refusal to drive, then about not having his bike.

I tuned him out, instead letting my mind wander over the problem we'd had in the lab that afternoon. The first test of our new tech, and it had been dead in the water. Not an unusual problem—these things rarely worked the first time. Was it the hardware or the software? My mind drifted over the code I'd written as we walked, my focus allowing me to ignore both Stuart's rambling and my pinched toes.

I heard the club before I saw it, the thumping dance music audible as the door opened and closed. Rounding a corner, we hit the tail end of a long line of men and women dressed a lot like I was, though they looked perfectly at home in their designer gear.

I couldn't stop tugging my skirt down or checking to make sure I hadn't fallen out of Emily's push-up bra. I was very curvy. The push-up bra was overkill, but she'd insisted the dress demanded cleavage. Well, cleavage I had. So much cleavage, I was tempted to ogle my own breasts. I normally didn't see this much of them outside of the shower.

Stuart led me past the line and past the two bouncers guarding the door, one studying the ID of a tall blonde girl, the other holding back a velvet rope to allow a brunette in a little black dress and her suited date to enter. In Emily's clothes, I'd blend in, but Stuart was going to stick out like a sore thumb with his kakis and elbow patches. We walked around the corner into a wide, well-lit alley. Halfway down the alley, there was a second entrance, with a single bouncer and no line. I held my breath, ready for Stuart's coin to be rejected.

The bouncer gave Stuart an indecipherable look as he examined the shiny gold coin, then slid it into his pocket. "ID," he said. We showed him our IDs, waiting while he flashed a light over them, making a point of giving special attention to Stuart's. When his eyes slid to me, they warmed with a smile and he gave me a friendly nod as he returned my license and stamped both of our hands. "You're good. Enjoy."

He opened the door and stepped back to allow us to enter. I forgot about Stuart, my aching feet and my software glitch. I forgot everything as we entered the dark of the club. Scents hit me, a swirl of perfume and alcohol, which blended with the pulse of music, enveloping us in the heart of the club. The lights were low, flashing every so often in time with the music, but I could see the interior of the club well enough. As I'd expected, it was filled with beautiful people, dancing and drinking as if they belonged there. The rest was a surprise.

I'd pictured something modern, shiny and new, with clean lines and sharp edges. Vaguely, I recalled hearing that the building had once been a church, then a theater. It explained why the central room soared above us, majestic and old world, with painted murals and gilt details on the ornate plaster. The club was at least four levels, and each one had balconies overlooking the main room. Taking in all the details, I followed Stuart past the bar to the side of the main room and up a flight of stairs. In the stairwell, the music dimmed enough for me to hear when Stuart shouted over his shoulder,

"The coin got us access to the VIP lounge on the third floor," he said, leading me up another flight of stairs.

I hoped he knew where he was going. We passed a few couples and a group of giggling girls on our trip from the main floor to the second, but once we reached the second floor, the stairwell had been empty. I was suddenly aware of being alone in the dark with a man I barely knew. Before I could decide what to do about that, we came to a stop in front of a heavy, tall, wooden door covered in ornate carvings that I could barely see in the dim light. Stuart hesitated before placing his palm on the polished surface and pushing it open.

CHAPTER TWO

JOSEPHINE

I STEPPED INTO THE DOORWAY OF THE VIP LOUNGE and almost stumbled as my path was blocked by a wall of a man with a chest that looked as wide as the doorway.

"Hand," he barked, his eyes scanning me, then Stuart. I showed him my hand, and he studied the stamp, then did the same to Stuart before stepping back in silence to allow us entry.

Again, the room defied my expectations. Polished, dark wood surrounded us—in the beams of the ceiling, the walls, and the long, packed bar. Plush leather chairs and couches filled the room, creating intimate seating areas, an oasis of elegance and calm. If the club-goers in the lower levels had been glamorous, those up here were a cut above. Everything about the VIP lounge said wealth and privilege.

This wasn't a place to be seen. This was where the elite went to relax with their own kind. Again, I wondered from whom Stuart had gotten his VIP invite. Neither of us belonged here, not even close. I planned to enjoy my visit to the other side as long as it lasted. If nothing else, I was going to have tons to tell Emily when I got home.

I let Stuart lead me to a loveseat in a corner, the only place to sit that wasn't already claimed. Sharing the small couch with Stewart wasn't my idea of a good time, but the alternative was standing, and not only did my feet hurt, but I didn't want to attract that kind of attention. I sat, hugging the arm of the loveseat furthest from Stewart, and tried to arrange my legs so they were nowhere near his.

A waitress in a little black dress appeared beside me. She was stunning, with long, sleek blonde hair and sharp cheekbones. Her dress was blatantly sexy, displaying her miles of toned leg and more than a hint of cleavage, but it wasn't trashy. Her look was class, from head to toe. Stuart ordered for both of us—a draft for him and a rum and diet coke for me. The waitress must have caught my scowl, or she had good instincts, because she raised her eyebrow at me after Stuart's order. I smiled at her in appreciation.

"A Bellini, please." I'd have to spring for an Uber after this, but even if I wasn't driving, I had no intention of getting drunk with Stuart. I loved champagne, but even when it was mixed with something, I always ended up sipping it. Not only did I not drink rum and diet anything, but I didn't want a strong drink.

Stuart eyed my legs and said, "I would have thought a girl like you would order something lighter."

I didn't respond. First of all, with the way he was leering at my legs, it was clear he found them attractive. And second, any man with manners bad enough to comment on the calorie level in my drink was beyond saving. I wasn't going to waste my one visit to the VIP lounge of the hottest club in town on trying to civilize Stuart. He was beyond help.

Resolved to ignore him, I took a sip of my Bellini and turned to check out the rest of the room. The VIP lounge was the perfect place to people watch. I started with the seating area adjacent to ours. It was larger, with a full-size couch and two wide arm chairs. The closest side of the couch was inches from where I sat, hugging the arm of our loveseat. The far side was occupied by a man with his back to me. In one of the arm chairs, a tall, slender blonde perched, leaning into the man, her hand on his leg and a seductive smile on her face. Sitting closer to me was another man, also facing the blonde. I couldn't see either of their faces, but both men had broad shoulders, long legs, and the same thick, dark hair.

Stuart's hand landed on my knee, his touch cool and a little clammy. Yuck. Drawing my legs back, I tucked them to the side, the position uncomfortable but far better than having his fingers on me. He sucked at his drink, the slurping sound audible in the tight space, and leaned closer, his eyes glued to my breasts. Double yuck. I started to wonder if experiencing the VIP lounge was worth putting up with Stuart.

Desperate to divert him, I said, "So, what were you saying before about the current limits on campaign donations and how they can be finessed?"

Stuart started to talk, and all I heard was, "Wahh, wahh, wahh." If our dinner was any indication, he'd be good for at least twenty minutes before he ran out of steam. Knowing he wouldn't notice, I looked around the room again. This time, as I turned my head, my eyes fell on the most beautiful man I'd ever seen. He was sitting on the end of the couch closest to me, his full lips quirked in amusement.

"Good one," he said, his low voice washing over me like warm honey. Dark eyes traveled my body slowly, making no effort to hide his appraisal. Unlike Stuart's leer, this man's look was all admiration. I crossed my legs, startled by the rush of heat between them from just a look.

"Excuse me?" I asked, watching him from the corner of my eye while keeping my face turned in Stuart's direction. The stranger gave a soft laugh.

"Please tell me this is a first date," he said, his voice quiet enough to avoid Stuart's attention. "You look way too smart to go out with this guy a second time."

I stifled a laugh and risked a quick turn of my head to meet his eyes, whispering, "Blind date. I almost left him at dinner when we split the check and he tried to stiff the waitress, but he had a VIP invite, and I've never been here before . . ." I trailed off, biting my lip.

I was constitutionally incapable of being cool. Oh, well. I was never one for pretending to be what I wasn't. Cool, at least the VIP level of cool, was beyond me. I shifted in my seat, angling my body toward the hot stranger as I turned my face back to Stuart. He was still rambling on about his dissertation and slurping at his drink, unaware I was talking to another man.

"Ouch," the stranger said. "How did a guy like that get a date with a woman like you? You're way out of his league."

I blushed. Feeling the heat in my cheeks, I blushed harder. I cleaned up well, but the make up and the short skirt weren't really me. This man was gorgeous. I'd bet he'd be gorgeous the morning after a bender, with no sleep, hungover. I took another quick look, one that ended up lingering as I took in his bladed cheekbones, deep brown eyes, and shining, thick hair the color of espresso. I couldn't see much of his body, but the length of his legs and the breadth of his shoulders hinted it would be worth getting a closer look.

The stranger beside me wasn't just some guy. He was a man. He lounged on the couch as if he owned the place, both commanding and at ease. I shifted in my seat as he tilted his head closer to mine, his warm breath on my cheek sending a pulse of need straight between my legs. I'd never reacted to a man like this, my body jumping to 'Go' before I knew his name. But as I mentioned, the man beside me was no 'guy'. He was more potent than any male I'd ever spoken to before. It was no wonder my body was overwhelmed.

His lips grazed my ear as he said, "Do you want to come sit over here?"

My jaw must have dropped. I *did* want to go sit over there. Could I? Just stand up and abandon my lackluster blind date? Before I could respond, I felt the stranger beside me shake his head. "No," he said. "Never mind. Let's just get out of here. I want to show you something."

I was still trying to catch up when he stood. Taking the step from his seating area to mine, he stopped before me, his hand extended. I stared up at him dumbly. I'd been right. His body was well worth a closer look. Looming above me, he filled my vision. I didn't think about it. I just put my hand in his larger one and let him pull me to my feet.

Off in the distance, through the buzzing in my ears, I heard a laugh and a female gasp, then caught the sound of Stuart sputtering a protest. The stranger had me caught in a spell, his dark gaze hot as he scanned my face, dipping only briefly to my exposed cleavage before locking on my eyes.

Pulling me closer, he said, "I know it's crazy, and completely inappropriate, but I've been wanting to do this since you walked in the door."

A sharp tug on my hand and I fell forward, closing the inches between us, my breasts pillowing against his hard chest. Startled, I looked up to see his face draw closer until his mouth came down on mine. I'd been kissed before—not a ton, but more than a few times. I'd never been kissed like this. His arm wrapped around my waist, pressing my body to his, turning me until my legs straddled his thigh. His hand closed over my hip with a possessive grip.

He didn't start slow. His lips hit mine, opening my mouth to him, his tongue stroking, teasing me, claiming me. If I'd thought about it, I'm sure I would have done something—backed away, protested, something. Anything other than what I did. I curled my fingers around his shoulders and held on for dear life while a complete stranger ravaged me with the kiss of a lifetime.

I'd stepped out of my boring blind date and into a dream. I'd never seen a man this hot in real life, much less been kissed by one. I didn't have it in me to shut him down. Maybe it was the margaritas at dinner or the pathetic excuse for a date. Maybe the stranger kissing me was just that hot. I didn't care. I kissed him back with everything I had, holding on tight, relishing the scrape of his stubble on my cheek and the heat of his lips moving on mine.

When he finally broke the kiss, I was panting. I may have been whimpering, just a little. His lips dropped to my ear, nipping the lobe for a second before he said, "Do you want to get out of here?"

Speech was beyond me. I nodded, my eyes on his, then on the floor. Now that we weren't kissing any longer, I couldn't bear to see the faces of the people around us. I'd kissed a complete stranger in a bar. And not a peck. That had been a full on, hand groping, tongues twining kiss. A panty soaking, *please, please take me somewhere and get me naked* kind of kiss.

My cheeks burned with embarrassment as I fumbled for my purse with one hand, the other firmly in the stranger's grip. I caught a glimpse of Stuart's outraged face as I was turned in the direction of the door. Behind me, I heard Stuart say, "You can't just take my date!"

He got no answer. I had no idea what to say, and apparently, my new date had deemed him unworthy of a response. I followed the stranger down the stairs and out into the alley, wondering what the hell I was doing leaving the club with a man I'd just met. I knew other women did this all the time, but I never had. Maybe it was my turn to loosen up a little and have some fun. I still couldn't believe I'd caught the eye of a man like this, and I wasn't going to ruin it by second-guessing myself.

I let the stranger lead me out of the alley and onto the street. He turned me back in the direction of the restaurant where I'd had dinner with Stuart. Dimly, I noted that moving in the direction of my car was probably a good thing. His voice interrupted the quiet, startling me out of my thoughts.

"What's your name?" he asked, releasing my hand so he could slide his arm around my shoulders.

"Josephine," I said. "Jo."

"Do you go by Josephine or Jo?" he asked.

"Mostly Jo," I said in a whisper, embarrassed by my tomboyish name. Normally, I liked it, but tonight, it didn't feel like it fit me.

"I like Josephine. You look like a Josephine." He must be a mind reader. Answering the question on my lips, he said, "I'm Holden."

"Do you usually steal women away from their dates?" I asked tartly, then flushed at my tone. He laughed, looking down at me. I was five feet, five inches tall—not short, but he towered above me. He must have been at least a few inches over six feet. He grinned at me and shook his head, saying, "Never. I can honestly say that I've never stolen a girl from her date in the VIP Room at Mana before."

"So you have stolen a woman from her date before? Just not there?" I asked in the same tart tone. I didn't know what was wrong with me, but his complete self-assurance made me want to poke at him, just a little.

"I may have broken up a date or two in the past," he confessed. "But I don't go to the VIP room to hook up. If I want a woman, I hit the club downstairs. The VIP room is for relaxing."

I started to make a sharp comment about the easy way he described the club as if it were an 'All You Can Eat' buffet. Sneaking a look at his chiseled profile, I shut my mouth. For him, it probably was. I bet most of the women in that club would have tripped over themselves—and their dates— if they thought Holden was interested in taking off their clothes. I was very aware of how wet my panties were after one kiss.

"So why me?" I asked before I could stop myself.

CHAPTER THREE

JOSEPHINE

*H*OLDEN DIDN'T ANSWER MY QUESTION. IT was just as well. Either he'd lie and tell me it was love at first sight or some bullshit like that, or he'd tell the truth, which would likely be unflattering, considering I was a girl who'd left a club with a complete stranger and was heading home with him. At least, I assumed that's where we were heading. *I thought you looked like an easy hook up* was probably closer to the truth, but it would put a huge damper on my mood.

Just as I was telling myself to stop overthinking, Holden stopped at the front door of an imposing brick building.

Winters House. I'd been here a few times. There was a funky coffee house on the first floor that made a killer latte, and it was close to campus. Did Holden live here? I'd heard there were apartments in the upper floors, above the retail and the offices, but I'd also heard they were huge, unbelievably expensive, and you practically had to sell your firstborn child to get one.

A horrible thought occurred to me. Holden looked older than me, but not old enough to own one of these places. Please tell me he didn't live with his parents. Never mind. I shoved that thought right out of my head. No way this guy lived at home. Maybe he was just taking me for coffee. After that kiss, I'd been sure we were headed straight to bed—and, margaritas aside, it was weird how cool I was with that—but what did I know? I didn't leave bars with strangers every day. Maybe he thought coffee and a scone came next.

I was wrong. Holden strode through the lobby with me beside him, ignoring the coffee house, the upscale boutique, and the art gallery, and headed directly for the elevators. Ushering me in before him, he pressed a button, then lay his palm on a flat, dark screen. A green line passed beneath his palm, up and down, then up again. The line vanished, and the elevator slid smoothly to the upper floors. I stared at Holden in disbelief.

"Was that a palm scanner?" I asked. I didn't spend a lot of time in high-end buildings, but a palm scanner seemed a little extreme. Holden shrugged.

"We take our security seriously," he said. "And certain people kept losing their keys." He scowled, and I had the feeling he was well-acquainted with the loser of the keys.

"So, you live here?" I asked, hesitant.

"Yep." He didn't offer any more information, and I didn't want to press. Actually, I did want to press, but the gleam in his dark eyes as he backed me into the corner of the elevator distracted me. I decided I didn't care if he still lived at home. All I cared about was getting those big, strong hands on me again.

I didn't have to wait long. Holden didn't stop until my back was pressed into the polished wood of the elevator wall, penning me in with his tall frame. I gasped in surprise when his hands closed around my waist and he lifted me, pinning me to the wall with his hips, one hand clamped on my ass. His lips found mine, and I was lost. It didn't occur to me to wonder if anyone else might get in the elevator or to worry that he'd tugged my dress down until my full breasts spilled free.

His hard cock pressed between my legs, only his jeans and my thin silk dress between us. I wrapped my legs around him, pulling him in deeper, grinding against him, moaning as my mouth drew on his and my tongue tasted him, my hands buried in his thick, silky hair.

Holden's hand on my ass had moved beneath my short skirt, pushing my panties aside until one long finger traced around my pussy. I surged against his finger, needing to feel him inside me, my sense of control completely lost. I had no clear idea where I was or what I was doing. I just wanted more of him.

"Holden." I gasped his name, squirming and grinding against him. I never noticed when the elevator stopped and the doors slid open. His mouth left mine, and he lifted me from the wall, carrying me, still kissing me, from the elevator.

"Fuck me, you're hot," he said in a growl, opening a door and pushing inside. We didn't get very far, no more than a few steps, before he set me down on a cool, hard surface. In the dim light, I thought we might be in a kitchen. Before I could look around, he unzipped my dress and whipped it over my head. I didn't have a second to get self-conscious. When he stepped back and started at me, the heat in his eyes made me dizzy.

"Take off your bra," he said, his gaze fixed on my breasts, barely contained by the thin, lacy bra. My hands trembling, I reached behind me and flicked open the clasp, letting the dark straps fall down my arms. The lacy cups hung for a moment on the tips of my beaded nipples before the wisp of fabric slipped free. I let the bra fall to the floor and braced my hands behind me, arching my back and offering my breasts to Holden.

He groaned deep in his throat and lunged forward, filling his hands with my breasts, his mouth on one nipple, teeth teasing me with tiny bites as his fingers pinched and twisted the other side. I wiggled my hips forward until they met his at the edge of the counter, wrapping my legs around him, needing to feel his hard length between my legs, even with my panties and his jeans between us.

Never, in my entire life, had I imagined desire like this. Holden was more than hot, and this was more than lust. I needed him—needed him inside me, his mouth on me, his cock fucking me. I wanted to beg, to demand, but I was too busy just trying to breathe.

He released my breasts and stepped back. I heard a snap of metal just before the rustle of his jeans hit the floor. Then, a sound I'd never heard before—fabric tearing as he ripped my lace panties to get to my pussy. As if I hadn't already been boiling over with desire, the feel of cool air on my wet pussy was almost more than I could take.

"Please, Holden," I whimpered. The head of his cock nudged my entrance, and I arched my hips, more than ready for him. Reality got in the way. "Wait," I said, almost sobbing with frustration.

"Fuck. Condom. Don't move," he ordered. Then he was gone. If he'd taken too long, I might have had time for my brain to kick into gear and remind me that I was naked in the kitchen of a man I didn't know, about to have sex with him. Fortunately for my sex-starved body, I didn't have time to do more than register how wet I was, how good his mouth had felt on my breasts, and how cold the marble countertop was against my heated skin before Holden was back.

He leaned into me, his chest hard against my nipples, his cock pressing into my pussy, stretching me open. Either he was huge, or in the year since I'd had sex, I'd magically become a virgin again. Based on his general size, I was guessing he had a big cock. Exact inches didn't matter. The only thing I cared about was the delicious feeling of him pushing his way inside me, setting every nerve in my pussy on fire, until he was buried to the hilt, his pelvic bone shoved right up against my swollen clit. Fuck me. I'd never felt anything this good.

Never. My breath sobbed out of my chest in gasps. I gripped his shoulders and held on as he began to pump his hips, fucking that thick cock into me in short, staccato thrusts that worked my clit exactly the right way.

I heard myself crying out as my first orgasm hit, barely a minute after he started to move, my voice keening and breathless. Holden rode me through the waves, then pulled out of me and lay me down on the counter, his mouth tracing a path from my breast to my shoulder to my neck before finding my lips.

His kiss was carnal. Obscene. His mouth took over, his tongue sliding against mine, his lips opening me, taking everything. When he fucked his cock back into me, it felt twice as big, and I was as desperate as if I hadn't come in months.

"Josephine," Holden breathed into my ear. "Fuck, Josephine, your pussy is so fucking tight."

I couldn't do anything but moan in response. His words were direct and so dirty, but the way he said my name . . . he drew it out like it was a song, or a prayer.

Josephine.

It had always felt too old-fashioned, but when Holden said it, it was exactly right.

"You feel so fucking good on my cock," he whispered in my ear. "I'm going to fuck you until you come all over me, sweet Josephine, and then I'm going to fucking fill you up."

A sound escaped my throat, something between a whimper and a plea. One of his big hands went to my lower back, lifting me and angling my pussy down as he thrust up, filling me another impossible inch. The head of his cock rubbed my G-Spot, the base of it ground into my clit, and the top of my head blew off as my second orgasm hit me in a blinding rush of bliss.

I may have passed out a little after that. The next thing I remember, Holden was carrying me to his bathroom. He set me down beside a huge white soaking tub and turned on the water. Steam billowed up, filling the room. With his hand on my back, he nudged me up the steps and into the tub, joining me after adding a generous squirt of something that smelled like oranges and sunshine.

Despite the size of the tub, it filled quickly. Normally, I would have minded getting my hair wet—it was long, thick, and took forever to dry—but I was so relaxed from two orgasms, I probably would have let Holden cut it all off. He settled us against the back of the tub, me between his spread legs, his half-hard cock against my lower back. My head lolled on his shoulder and his hands rested on my ribs, his fingertips teasing the underside of my breasts.

"So, do you go out on a lot of blind dates?" he asked, as if picking up our earlier conversation in the VIP room of Mana.

"Mmm, not really. That was a favor to my advisor," I admitted. "Her nephew."

"Is that going to be a problem for you?" he asked. Trying to get my sleepy, aroused brain in gear, I thought about his question.

"I don't think so," I said. "She's pretty cool." I thought about the way we'd left—me kissing Holden right in front of

Stuart, then walking out without a word to my date. "I guess it depends on what he tells her."

Before I could start stressing about what Stuart might say to my advisor, Holden asked, "What's she advising you in?"

"I'm a grad student," I explained, "at Tech." I gave him the short version of what I was studying. It was pretty specialized, and most people were good with me leaving out the details. I can't remember how much I told him. His fingers started trailing across my breasts, drawing designs on my skin with water and suds until I forgot I'd been talking at all.

He turned me over, shifting my body until I was straddling him, my face tucked into his neck. I loved his body, the size of him, the way I fit against him. I wasn't a small girl, and Holden didn't seem huge, but he was big enough to make me feel delicate, and that was a feat.

He must have put a condom by the side of the tub, because he was suited up and sliding inside me a moment later. I ground down on him, taking every inch, rocking and sliding as his strong hands gripped my ass. When the orgasm started to rise, I sank my teeth into his shoulder to hold back my scream.

"God, baby. Yes. Fuck my cock, Josephine. Fuck me hard."

I did as I was told, losing control, water splashing to the floor as I chased my orgasm. My pussy clamped down hard, my release milking Holden dry.

I don't remember how we got from the tub to his bed. Somewhere along the way, he dried me off and tucked me between sheets so smooth, I thought they couldn't possibly be cotton. I passed out with my head on his chest, his arm holding me close.

I only woke once, in the early morning, to find myself flat on my back, my legs spread with Holden between them. As if we'd been fucking for years instead of hours, I lifted my legs and wrapped them around his hips, my mouth meeting his in a soft, slow kiss. That time, he took me gently, taking his time, his hands stroking me everywhere. I fell back asleep after we came, curled into him, every breath drawing in his woodsy, male scent.

***

I WOKE TO BLINDING SUNLIGHT in my half-open eyes. Squinting, I rolled over, trying to figure out where I was. Not my bedroom. I had a tiny window that faced away from the sunrise—one of my favorite things about my apartment. Blinking my stinging eyes, I sat up, feeling my stomach roll. The wave of nausea brought everything back.

Stuart. The awful date. Meeting Holden. Going home with Holden. Oh my God, had I seriously gone home with a strange guy and slept with him? Three times? I didn't know whether to be ashamed or proud of myself. I'd never done anything like this in my entire life. I jumped out of the bed like a scalded cat and retreated to the other side of the room, staring at the body between the smooth, heavy sheets in a combination of fascination and horror.

In sleep, Holden looked even hotter than my blurry brain remembered. He lay on his stomach, arms and legs splayed, like a child. His body belonged to a man—honey gold skin stretched over defined shoulders and a well-muscled back. His feet stuck out beneath the sheets at the end of the bed, and even his toes were hot—as tan as the rest of his skin, with little golden hairs. He looked perfect.

Had I really slept with that man? I remembered the way he'd laid me out on the kitchen counter and fucked me until I'd come twice. The stretch of his cock pressing into my body was burned into my brain. I hadn't just slept with him. I'd fucked him three times, begging for it, screaming when I came. My cheeks burned at the memory.

What was I doing? Why was I still there? This was a one-night stand. I wasn't supposed to stay. I was supposed to sneak out and never see him again. At that thought, my stomach clenched and I felt like throwing up. But that was just the hangover, right? I didn't even know the guy. Other than his first name, I knew nothing about him. Well, his first name and that he was fabulous in bed. And sweet, I thought, remembering the way he'd held me in the tub and as we'd slept.

I shouldn't leave. It was rude to sneak out. Maybe he wanted me to stay. I was wavering until he shifted in the bed and rolled over. At the thought that he was waking up, that he might be about to open those dark eyes and look at me with disgust or disinterest, I crept out of the room as fast as I could. The night before had been amazing. Mind blowing. I couldn't stand the thought that he might look at me with regret . . . or worse, disappointment.

Moving as quickly as I could, I made my way back to the kitchen, where I discovered that Holden hadn't fucked me on the counter. It had been a huge, white, marble-topped island, and my dress was still puddled in the center, beside a wooden bowl of fresh fruit.

Still life with abandoned dress.

I shuddered and grabbed it, yanking it over my head as soon as I had my bra snapped. At least I'd dropped all my clothes in the same place. Slipping my sore feet into Emily's torture chamber shoes, I located my purse on its side, half the contents spilled out onto the floor. Hastily, I shoved everything back in and snuck out the door, praying the elevator didn't need a handprint to let me out. It didn't.

I slung my purse over my shoulder and walked into the lobby, my head held high, shoulders back. This was my very first walk of shame, but I wasn't going to actually *be* ashamed.

I wasn't.

Okay, so I'd slept with a guy I didn't know. Not my best move. But there was nothing wrong with it. People did it all the time. It was over, and no one had to know.

I headed out of the building, ignoring the enticing scent of coffee filling the first level. I didn't dare linger at the scene of the crime. Not that I thought Holden was coming after me. When he woke up, he'd probably be relieved I was gone.

CHAPTER FOUR

HOLDEN

*J*ROLLED OVER AND STRETCHED MY ARM ACROSS THE bed, reaching for something. When my fingers encountered only cool, smooth sheets, my eyes opened, and I stared at the ceiling, waiting for my brain to come back online.

What had I been reaching for? Rolling over, I caught sight of the indented pillow, smelled sex in my bed, and remembered. Josephine. I was reaching for Josephine.

I had no idea what time it was. My phone hadn't made it to the nightstand, and I didn't have a clock in the bedroom.

I didn't have to check the time to know she was gone. The apartment felt too empty. Fuck.

Fuck.

I rarely brought women back to my place. Tate, my cousin who owned the other apartment on this floor, brought women home all the time. It wasn't the weekend if I didn't run into one of his giggling, half-drunk party girls stumbling to his door.

Personally, I didn't like dealing with the morning after shit. When women got a good look at where I lived, they usually started angling to stay—offering to make me breakfast or fuck me all weekend. To be fair, it wasn't just the apartment. Most of them already knew who I was. No Winters can keep a low profile in this town. My family has been making the news since well before I was born. Nothing gets attention like a ton of money wrapped up in scandal.

That was one of the things I liked about Josephine. It was clear she had no idea who I was. She was an innocent, her blue eyes wide as she'd walked into Mana with her dipshit date. She'd caught my attention the second she crossed the threshold, and not just because I'd been bored and annoyed with Tate's date for the night.

Josephine had easily been the most beautiful woman there. That body. Fuck. Her dress had been elegant and sexy, but not blatant. On a different woman, the dress might have even been subdued. Not on Josephine. Her body was all curves, from her shapely legs to her round ass to her luscious tits. I could have spent all day worshipping those tits. She had pale skin for a blonde. When she'd been naked, spread out on the marble of my kitchen island, she'd been a lush work of art, straight out of the Renaissance.

Fucking gorgeous. I'd wanted to smack her date when he'd made a comment about her weight. Calling him a moron was an insult to morons. How he could look at a body like Josephine's and think she needed to change a God dammed thing was beyond me. Everything about her was perfect.

And her pussy. At the thought of her pussy, my mouth watered and my cock came to full attention. God damn, she'd had the tightest, sweetest pussy I'd fucked in as long as I could remember. The way she came for me, so easily, her cunt scalding hot and clenching down on my cock as she'd screamed.

Fuck.

It started to hit me that she was really gone. I'd never wanted to see a hookup the next day. I was usually the one sneaking out. I would have thought I'd be grateful the girl I'd picked up had taken off. If it had been any other girl, I would have been. But I'd fallen asleep with the taste of Josephine in my mouth, and waking up alone sucked. I didn't even know her last name.

Irritation flooded through me, and I dragged myself out of bed and headed for the shower, half-hoping I'd turn out to be wrong and she'd still be around somewhere. When I emerged from the shower to the scent of freshly brewed coffee, I was a little embarrassed at the surge of eagerness in my chest. Maybe I'd been wrong, and she was still here.

The look on my face when I saw Tate sitting at my kitchen island must have been amusing, because he laughed and said, "What, expecting someone else?"

I pulled up a stool and sat at the island, hunched over my elbows, suddenly cranky, hungry, and wishing I were alone.

"Fuck you," I said without heat. "How is it that you constantly lose your keys, but you always manage to unlock *my* door?"

A full, steaming mug of coffee slid under my nose. I picked it up and took a sip, the taste of fresh coffee chasing away some of the cobwebs.

"So," Tate said, waiting until I'd finished most of my first cup. "Spill. Where's the girl? Don't tell me you didn't break your rule and bring her back here. I saw that kiss. If you weren't a legend with the staff before, you are now."

"Fuck you," I repeated, knowing I'd end up telling Tate everything. Not quite everything. He didn't need to know the details of how amazing Josephine was. If I ever managed to track her down, I didn't want competition from my cousin. Not that he would do that to me. Shit, I was in a bad mood.

"I'm not leaving until you tell me everything," he said. I let out a sigh and finished my coffee.

"Tell me you brought food," I grumbled, getting up to refill my mug from the vacuum carafe on the counter.

"In the oven," Tate said, sliding his mug toward me. I poured his coffee and opened the oven door. The scents of bread, cheese, and bacon wafted out, and my stomach growled. The coffee house downstairs not only had fantastic coffee, but they made amazing breakfast sandwiches. Since we lived on the tenth floor and had our offices on the fourth, Tate and I ate there a lot. I grabbed an oven mitt and retrieved our breakfast. Ignoring Tate, I sat back on my stool and dug in. He did the same.

"At least tell me you broke your rule and brought her home," Tate said when he was done. I swallowed the last bite of my sandwich and brushed my hands off on my jeans, finally feeling awake.

"I did," I admitted. Tate let out a shout of glee.

"I knew it. How was she?" he asked, eyebrows raised. "She looked wound tight, but sometimes, those are the best when you get them naked."

I stayed silent. Tate wasn't trying to be an asshole. We didn't go into extreme detail about the women we fucked, but we were tight, and we had more than our share of hook-ups. Normally, I'd say something like, *she was fuckin' amazing*, he'd say, *right on*, and we'd change the subject.

I opened my mouth to play the game and found the words stuck in my throat. For the first time in my life, I understood what *fucking amazing* truly meant. Josephine had been the best fuck of my life because it was more than a fuck. I don't know how, since I barely knew her, but last night had been more than just sex. I dropped my head to stare at the marble countertop. Fuck.

"What?" Tate asked. "Don't tell me it was bad. I saw that kiss. Half the girls in the room were wet by the time you left. She was hot as fuck."

Yeah, she was. I opened my mouth to say something, then shut it. Finally, I said, "She was perfect, and when I woke up this morning, she was gone."

Tate stared at me, his mouth hanging open, his eyes wide. After a pause, he recovered from his shock and said carefully, "And this is a problem?"

"Yes," I said, my voice tight, eyes still on the counter. "This is a problem. She snuck out in the middle of the night. I don't have her last name, her number, anything."

Tate shrugged. "Does it matter? It was just a hook-up, right? I can't imagine you had that much time to talk."

"We didn't do a lot of talking," I admitted. We hadn't.

So why did I care that she'd taken off? Because the sex was that good? It had been, but was that enough of a reason to go chasing after some girl? "I still want to find her," I said.

"You sure?" Tate asked. "We'll track her down if you want to, but think about it first. Do you really want to get yourself tied up in knots over some girl? What are the chances this is going to be anything other than just sex?"

I pushed off my stool and paced the kitchen, letting Tate's words run through my head. I knew what he was getting at. Winters men did not have good luck with relationships. Only one of us, my oldest brother, Aiden, had been married, and he was two years divorced at thirty-two. We were notorious: wealthy, powerful, and cursed. Love was a complication every one of us had avoided. Even Aiden had married more for practicality than any emotion.

My night with Josephine had been spectacular, but let's be honest. I could get sex—amazing sex—any time I wanted it. What was so special about *her*? I barely knew her. I definitely didn't know her well enough to risk opening myself up to the pain of a relationship. All of us had been through too much loss too young. We played things loose as adults. Winters men worked hard, had fun, and were loyal only to each other. It kept us safe and whole. If I were smart, I'd forget about Josephine, chalk the night up to a great memory, and move on.

"You're right," I said, bringing my empty mug to the carafe, snagging Tate's along the way. "It's not a big deal."

I refilled our mugs and handed Tate his as he said, "Did you look over the report on the new physics engine?"

"I did," I said, trying to switch gears to work. "I'm not surprised it's running behind. We scheduled it that way, knowing it would hit some snags. But I think you're right. We might consider delaying development of Syndrome 2 a few months so we can incorporate the new features. The graphics would be unbelievable if we used the new engine."

"It won't be ready for GDC," he said, referring to the Game Developers Conference.

I shrugged. "We have enough buzz without it."

Tate and I had branched off from Winters Enterprises' typical investments in business—real estate, shipping, and emerging resources—to start a gaming company. So far, we'd mainly built games, but in the last year, we'd begun development on a new physics engine that would change gaming as we knew it. Once we got the bugs worked out, we'd be able to license the engine to other developers, as well as use it in our own games. Both creatively and financially, it would be a massive coup.

So massive, I really should have been able to keep my mind on our conversation. Instead, all I could think about was Josephine. I'd fucked her right there on the marble island. She'd been so fucking tight and sweet. I'd never be able to look at my kitchen without thinking of her hot pussy clamping down on my cock, milking my orgasm from me as she screamed her release. I shook my head, trying to chase off the memory.

I was not going to go chasing after a one-night stand. It was only asking for trouble. I'd forget the way we'd slept together, the way she'd curled into me, her long, blonde hair streaming over my chest, her soft breasts pressed against my skin. The way she'd smelled, sweet and clean, how she'd curled her fingers around my arm as she'd drifted off, holding me close in sleep. It didn't mean anything.

"You're thinking about her, aren't you?" Tate asked. I looked over to see his sharp blue eyes narrowed on my face. No one knew me like Tate. We were born three months apart and looked enough alike that people often mistook us for twins. We'd lived a charmed life when we'd been too young to remember it. By the time we were five, and everything fell apart, we'd learned to stick together. As the youngest males in the Winters clan, Tate and I had been a team. He knew what was on my mind almost as soon as the thought formed. It was useless to try to hide anything from him—what he didn't sense, he'd pry out of me.

"Yeah," I admitted. "I can't really explain it. I know I don't know her. I know we just fucked. But I can't leave it like this. Maybe I'll find her, take her out, and it doesn't work. I can live with that. But I have to know."

Tate shifted gears from trying to talk me out of going after Josephine. He knew me well enough to sense when he'd be wasting his time. And true to Tate, he was loyal, first, last, and always. He'd done his best to talk sense into me, and now that I was determined to go over the cliff, I'd do it with him at my back.

"So," he said, getting practical. "What did you find out about her? Atlanta isn't that big. We can find one woman."

I laughed. Tate was right. Not about Atlanta not being big. It was a city of five and a half million people. One woman could easily disappear into the masses. Except I was a Winters. This was my city, and I had resources. If I really wanted to find Josephine, she wouldn't be able to hide from me for long.

"She's a grad student at Tech," I said. "CS, HCI specialization. She has a car, so she might not live nearby."

Tate whistled. "At least you picked a smart one," he said. "Does she know what you do?"

I shook my head. "We never even got to last names."

"Then call Cooper," Tate said, as if it were just that simple. Actually, it could be just that simple. Cooper Sinclair was like an older brother. All the Sinclairs were. We'd grown up together, and they were the closest thing to family we had outside the Winters clan. They also ran one of the best private security companies in the US, and their main offices were based in Atlanta. If I called Cooper, or one of his brothers, they could probably find Josephine for me before lunch. They'd also give me shit about it until the day I died.

I didn't mind that. Not really. Giving and getting shit was a key part of male bonding. Growing up with brothers and male cousins, plus all the testosterone in the Sinclair family, I knew how to take shit without getting bent out of shape. Hell, even my baby sister, Charlie, could dish it out. My gut told me that finding Josephine would be worth a ribbing from Cooper and the rest of the guys. What held me back wasn't my pride. It was more about self-protection.

I didn't know Josephine as well as I'd like to, but I sensed she was not the kind of girl who would take the Winters lifestyle in stride. We were high-profile to begin with, and that was only considering the media, business, and factors outside the family. We were also interfering as hell and nosy in the extreme.

Tate and I were the most laid back in the family. I always thought that came from being so young when shit went bad. Charlie was younger than us, but as the only girl, she felt she had too much to prove to relax. I could only imagine what would happen if word got out that I was interested in a woman. Just the thought of Charlie grilling her on her intentions gave me a chill.

Remembering the look in her eyes as she'd walked into the VIP room at Mana, the wonder and the nerves, I knew I'd have to ease her into everything that came with dating a Winters. She didn't even know Tate and I owned the club. If I called in Cooper, she'd be tossed straight into the deep end. She'd already run on me once. If I wanted to keep her, I'd have to play this nice and slow.

"I'd rather avoid Cooper if I can," I said to Tate. "I'm better off keeping Josephine under the radar."

Tate gave me a short nod. I didn't need to explain to him. "Let's head down to the office for a few hours and check last night's run. Maybe we'll think of something," he said.

"Good idea." I grabbed my wallet and keys off the counter and headed to the front door to find my shoes. I had a regular cleaning team, but they couldn't do anything about the crap I left lying around the place. They cleaned, but they didn't pick up after me. I found my shoes right where I expected, kicked off beside the front door. Leaning over, I reached for one and spotted a scrap of paper crumpled beneath the bench. My heart thumped in my chest as I picked it up and smoothed the paper flat. In handwriting I didn't recognize, it said,

Su. 3:30 Son. Lab

Reading it again, triumph surged in my chest. This was Josephine's. It had to be. I knew it wasn't mine, and no one else had been in the apartment since the cleaners except Tate. Just in case, I handed the note to him. He read it and shook his head.

"Not mine. You think Su is Sunday?"

"No idea." It looked like a note reminding her of a meeting. Probably on campus, given the word 'lab' in the description. Pulling my phone from my pocket, I opened the browser and typed in: *GA Tech son lab*

The first result was *Georgia Tech Sonification Lab: an interdisciplinary research group based in the School of Psychology and the School of Interactive Computing at Georgia Tech*. Fuck yeah. If Su meant today, I knew where I could find my girl.

Fate could be a bitch, but if I were lucky, she loved me today.

CHAPTER FIVE

JOSEPHINE

I RUSHED DOWN THE CONCRETE AND BRICK SIDEWALK on Cherry Street, my eyes on my feet, ignoring everything around me. I was hung over. A shower and breakfast had brought me from miserable to moderately human, but I still felt like crap, and I'd had a knot in my stomach ever since I'd left Holden's place that morning. I'd run out of there like a thief, and I hadn't done anything wrong. I'd gone home, hoping Emily would tell me I'd done the right thing, but she'd shaken her head and said I should have stayed.

"Jo-Jo," she'd said, "when was that last time either of us met a decent guy? Holden sounds like a fairy tale. You should have at least gone back for one more roll in the sheets before running off like the ho you are."

I'd thrown a pillow at her and escaped into the shower. Her teasing had struck a nerve. I should have stayed. I was trying to shake it off—nothing I could do about it now. I didn't even know his last name. *You know where he lives*, I reminded myself. True. I did know where he lived. But the vision of hanging around in the coffee house in his building, hoping to catch a glimpse of him, was too pathetic for me to consider. At least, not yet.

Annoyed with myself, I pushed thoughts of Holden from my mind and walked faster. I was never late to lab, but between my hangover and throwing pillows at my roommate, I'd have to run to get there by three. Since there was no way I was running anywhere with my post-hangover headache, I picked up my pace and prepared to be a few minutes late.

"Jo!" I turned my head to the familiar voice calling my name and slowed my pace to let my teammate, Darren, catch up. "Damn you're walking fast," he said. "It won't kill you to be a few minutes late."

I shrugged. "I know. It's a habit."

"I think Angie wishes you'd rub off on the rest of us."

I laughed. Angie was the leader of our project, and she made me look like a slacker. She probably did wish my habitual punctuality would rub off on the rest of the group. All of us were smart—you didn't get into our program or this research project without being very smart—but we all had a habit of getting caught up in our work and forgetting meetings and deadlines. I had a thing about programming alarms into my phone each morning to force me to stay on schedule. Without that, I'd be perpetually late like Darren.

"So what's your vote?" Darren asked as we walked. "Hardware or software?"

In between my awful date and my erotic dream of a night with Holden, I'd been mulling over this exact question. "I'm voting for both."

"Oh, she goes for the hard shot," Darren said in exaggerated dismay. I laughed and nudged him with my shoulder.

"I think we need to re-check the placement of the device on the glasses, but I also think I messed up the code in the interface."

"Not possible," Darren said, laughing.

"Very possible."

We were working on a project to help the vision impaired—a pair of glasses that could perform spatial mapping and communicate obstacles via Bluetooth to the user's phone. If we could get it to work, it could replace canes for the blind.

If we can get it to work.

The bridge between theory and execution was the most complicated part of developing new tech. I hadn't been surprised when we'd fired up the glasses the day before and gotten a dead screen, but I'd still been disappointed.

We rounded the corner to the door of the building, and I came to a dead stop. Lounging on a bench beside the main entry to the Psychology building was Holden.

He got to his feet in a fluid, predatory surge that sent a hot tingle straight between my legs. He paced toward me, his hair gleaming in the sun, his tall frame athletic and graceful, the muscles in his broad shoulders apparent beneath his worn t-shirt. Yum.

I was crazy. I had to be crazy, because instead of waking the man and doing deliciously naughty things to his body all morning, I'd run away like a coward. How had he found me? I opened my mouth to ask, but the hot look in his dark eyes stopped my words.

I was suddenly aware I was not the girl he'd met the night before. Gone were the spike heels, designer dress, and artfully arranged curls. Standing before the most beautiful man I'd ever seen, I was wearing worn jeans, a t-shirt that said *Reaver's Barbecue* from my favorite sci-fi TV show, and the ubiquitous hoodie, this one in navy blue. My hair was in a messy bun held up by takeout chopsticks, and I didn't have on an ounce of makeup. Not even lip balm. I was shocked that Holden recognized me.

"Excuse me?" Darren said, startling me out of my shock. Holden had come to a stop directly in front of us, and I was staring up at him, jaw dropped, eyes wide. "Who are you?" Darren demanded, moving as if to shield me from Holden. Holden blocked him easily, sliding between us and curling his arm around me.

"Is this guy bothering you, Jo?" Darren asked, sounding like he was ready to start something with Holden.

I shook off my daze and said, "No, I'm good. I'll meet you inside." Darren made as if to lay a hand on Holden, and I said, "Really, Darren, I'm good. I'll see you in the lab in a minute."

Darren scowled at Holden for a moment, then left. At a loss for anything meaningful to say, I asked, "How did you find me?"

Holden reached into his back pocket and produced a familiar wrinkled note. I remembered my purse, open and on its side beneath the bench. I took the note from his fingers and glanced at it. "Good detective work," I said. Holden plucked the note from my fingers and put it back in his pocket.

"Why did you leave this morning?" he asked.

"I thought you'd want me to," I said.

"Really?" he asked, his eyes studying mine, demanding honesty.

"I was afraid you'd want me to leave," I admitted. Holden lifted his hands to cup my face, tilting my chin up to him.

"I didn't. I wanted you to stay."

"Oh," I whispered.

"Did you want to stay?" Holden asked quietly.

"Yes," I whispered again.

"Good." His lips brushed mine in a feather-light kiss that sent electric tingles straight to my nipples. Another brush, and I thought he had a direct line to my clit. When he slanted his mouth down on mine, claiming me in our second, very public kiss, I fell into him, kissing him back with everything I had. I'd been a fool to walk out on him, but now that I had a second chance, I wasn't going to blow it.

I have no idea how long we kissed. When we finally broke apart, Holden slid his thumb over my lower lip and ordered, "Have dinner with me tonight."

"Okay," I said.

"Seven? I'll pick you up."

"Okay." I gave him my address and my number, my head still spinning from that kiss. I turned to go into the building, then stopped. "Wait! What's your name? I mean, your whole name?"

"Winters. Holden Winters."

***

"HOLDEN WINTERS?" EMILY SHRIEKED. I stared at her in amazement. Emily was not a shrieker.

"What? Do you know him?" I asked, confused.

"Not personally, no," she said, shaking her head. "Sometimes, I forget you're not from here." She opened her laptop and started typing. A search results page popped up with pictures of Holden and a long list of web pages mentioning him. I saw the club, Mana, something about WGC, and lower down, headlines with the words murder, tragedy, and suicide. All of a sudden, I realized I was way over my head.

"I'm not spying on him," I said, looking away from the screen. "Just tell me what I need to know."

"Okay. First, you have to tell me—is he really that gorgeous in real life?"

"Yeah," I said.

"Damn," Emily sighed. "Okay, this is a sad story, and if it wasn't mostly common knowledge, I wouldn't tell you. But he may assume you know anyway now that he told you his name . . ." She trailed off.

"Just tell me, Em!"

"Okay, so the Winters family are old Atlanta. In our parents' generation, there were two brothers. I can't remember their names. They all lived in this huge estate in Buckhead. Big money."

I didn't need her to add the last part. I'd only been in Atlanta a few years, but I knew an estate in Buckhead meant big money.

"When I was a baby, so your Holden was probably a little kid, one of the brothers and his wife died in a murder/suicide. It was a huge scandal, really ugly. The kids—I think they had three or four boys—went to live with the other brother and his wife. Then, like ten years ago, the other brother and his wife were both killed in a break-in. But there were rumors that it wasn't really a break-in, but that it was another murder/suicide."

"Oh my God," I said, letting out a breath I hadn't known I'd been holding. "So his parents are dead?"

"I don't know which side of the family he's from, but either way, yeah. I remember the media was awful. I was too young for the first murders, but I was about eleven the second time, and it was horrible. The media followed the kids everywhere—they couldn't stop picking the whole thing apart. I still remember seeing a picture of all the kids at the funeral, the oldest boys trying to look strong. One of the youngest boys—they looked like twins, so I don't know if it was Holden or his cousin—was hugging a girl who'd been about my age. The only girl. Charlotte, I think. Or Caroline. Something with a 'C'. She was sobbing, and he held on to her so tightly. It was sad."

"Did they ever catch the killer?" I asked, my voice thick in my throat. I couldn't imagine losing my family like that, to such sudden violence, and then having to grieve under a microscope. I understood why it had stuck in Emily's head. She'd been through her own nightmare at a young age, part of it at the callous hands of the media. Seeing the family, kids her age, subjected to such violating attention at what had to be the worst time of their lives would have made an indelible impression on her.

She shook her head. "No, I don't think they did. They must have looked hard. The Winters family has the kind of clout that can turn the world upside down. The oldest son took over the business and became head of the family. I'm sure he pushed to solve the case. But as far as I know, they never found anything."

I sat in silence, trying to absorb what I'd learned as Emily flipped back open her laptop and started clicking.

"Did you know he owns Mana?" She asked. Dumbly, I shook my head. "And he runs WGC—the gaming company—with his cousin, Tate. I bet WGC is Winters Gaming Corp, or Company. Something like that. Holy shit, they still look like twins." Fanning herself, she rotated the laptop to show me a picture of Holden and his cousin at what looked like a tech conference, both in suits, grinning and gesturing toward a huge screen in front of a crowd. Good God, they were hot.

"He owns the club?" I asked. It explained how comfortable he was there. My head was spinning a little from the overload of information.

"And WGC. I heard a rumor they were working on a new physics engine. I'd love to get a look at that. If you guys keep going out, will you ask if I can see it?"

"One thing at a time," I cautioned. I was way out of my league with Holden Winters. Way out. "Let me get through dinner tonight before I start asking him for favors."

"Yeah, good point. Still, I heard that on top of the physics engine, they've got a team working on something new in emergent gaming for Syndrome 2. But that's only a rumor."

Emily's vision unfocused as she got lost in speculation of gaming technology. She was a fellow grad student in the CS department at Tech, but her focus was on gaming. With a dual concentration on interactive intelligence and graphics, Emily's research projects tended to fall in line with the same kind of work Holden's company did. It was no surprise she was distracted.

"Hey," I said, clapping my hands under her nose. "Focus, please. I have less than an hour before he's going to be here, my hair is a mess, and I'm not wearing any makeup. I need serious help."

Emily sat up and gave me her full attention. She was the best friend ever. Scanning me, she narrowed her eyes, cocked her head to the side, then said, "Loose hair with a little product to smooth it out, because you want to go casual after last night, and we don't have time for more. I'll do your makeup, but I'm going to go light. The jeans you wore Friday—they make your ass look great—and my plum batwing top. Casual but sexy."

"Jeans and light makeup?" I asked, biting my lip. The night before, I'd been rocking serious glamour. I couldn't go out with him wearing jeans and only a little makeup.

"Jeans and light makeup," Emily said firmly. "Trust me. He saw you on your way to lab, didn't he?"

I nodded.

"And he asked you out? Then kissed you on the sidewalk?"

I nodded again.

"You weren't the height of fashion this afternoon, and he still asked you to dinner. He probably saw you coming up the street. I bet he had plenty of time for a quick getaway. Trust me. He doesn't want some glamor girl. He wants you."

CHAPTER SIX

JOSEPHINE

THE DOORBELL RANG, AND I PRAYED EMILY WAS RIGHT. When she was finished with my makeup and putting product in my hair, I looked pretty good, but I definitely wasn't glamorous. For one thing, the jeans and batwing shirt were flattering, but I was not skinny like all those girls at Mana. Though Holden had seemed to like my curves.

Telling myself to stop obsessing, I went to answer the door. Emily was nowhere to be seen. I'm sure she wanted to check Holden out, but she was so shy, she tended to avoid meeting new people if at all possible, even when they were as hot as Holden Winters.

Taking a deep breath to steady myself, I unlocked the door and pulled it open. Holden stood there in the same jeans he'd worn that afternoon and an untucked blue button-down shirt. As always seemed to happen when I looked at him, I temporarily lost the power of speech. He stared down at me, then said, "Are you ready to go?"

I nodded and turned to grab my purse and keys from beside the door. Holden took my arm with his, leading me down the hall to the elevator.

"I thought I'd cook you dinner at my place," he said. "But if you'd rather go out, we can do that too."

"No," I said, "dinner at your place sounds good." His arm tucked through mine, and the heat of his body beside me brought back vivid memories of all the things he'd done to me at his place. I was more than happy to go back there. I wondered for a second if he would think I was too easy.

"I promise," he said, "I won't ravage you until after dessert."

"You don't have to wait that long," I said with a laugh, deciding I didn't really care if he thought I was easy. I'd slept with him the first night we met, and not only couldn't I take that back, but I didn't want to. There was nothing I regretted about the night before except running out on him after I'd woken up.

"Well," he said, dipping his head to bite the side of my neck as the elevator doors closed, "Maybe I'll ravage you once before dessert. Or between courses."

I shivered.

"We can play it by ear," I said, smiling inwardly and wishing we were already at his place.

As we left the building, he said, "It's a nice night, so I walked over. I hope you don't mind."

"No. I like walking." I did, and it was a perfect spring night—cool, but not cold, the warmth of the afternoon lingering in the air. Around us, people strolled, heading out to dinner or just enjoying the evening. With my arm tucked through Holden's, I was mostly oblivious to everyone else. He held me close, his touch teasing my body.

It had been a long, long time since I'd had sex before Holden, and my body wanted more. Not just more orgasms, but more Holden. No man had ever made me feel this way, so instantly hot, so seduced with just a touch. Interrupting my thoughts, he said,

"Did you have a good afternoon?"

I considered. "Yes and no," I said honestly. "Seeing you was good. The lab was not. We can't figure out why our project isn't working, and I have a bad feeling the problem is my code. I've been over it and over it, but I can't spot the bug."

"Can you tell me what you're working on?"

It was a reasonable question. There were projects that were confidential. If he ran WGC, he knew all about confidential tech. As Emily had mentioned, they were currently working on two projects that the gaming world would love to know about.

"I can, a little." Trying not to bore him to death, I explained about the spatial mapping glasses and helping the blind navigate without a cane.

"How does the phone communicate obstacles?" Holden asked, sounding interested.

"Right now, we're working on a kind of Morse code in vibrations. We've got a consult from linguistics helping us work out the best way to communicate non-verbally."

"Very cool," he said. "How do you know the problem is your code?"

"I don't. It could be the hardware. But the issue is in the connection between the glasses and the phone. We're using Bluetooth, and I wrote that part of the app. We can't get it to connect. Of all the problems . . ." I shook my head in frustration.

"I know. I always get more pissed when the bug is something basic. How many times do you connect with Bluetooth?"

"Exactly," I said, gratified that he got why I was so pissed. "My headphones link up automatically. It should be the spatial mapping causing the problem, not the Bluetooth. We're going to connect a phone with hardwire so we can work on that while I try to debug the app."

I was surprised to realize we were already at Holden's building. Of all the things I'd imagined for our date, a conversation about my work hadn't been one of them. I realized I was a little shallow, expecting that someone as hot and rich as Holden wouldn't have a brain. Given that he owned and ran both a successful nightclub and a gaming company, I should have known better. I watched him do the palm print thing to get the elevator working and said, "I'm guessing you don't have many uninvited guests."

"No, not many. Unless they're family. They show up uninvited all the time."

Guilt hit me as we entered his apartment. I'd looked him up, talked about him with Emily, and now I knew all these personal things about him. It felt invasive and wrong. Suddenly uncomfortable, I stepped away from him and blurted out, "Emily told me who you are. I mean, about your family, and that you own the club and WGC."

Holden shrugged, his mouth tight. "I was going to tell you," he said. "It's not a secret."

"I wasn't trying to pry." Holden looked so uncomfortable,

I felt terrible for saying anything. "I'm sorry about your family." I had to stop talking without thinking. I worried that I'd made things worse, but his mouth softened and he said,

"It was a long time ago."

"I'm still sorry."

"So am I. But the rest of my family is pretty tight. We got through it."

I wondered if you could ever really get over such loss, but I managed to keep my mouth shut. Mostly. "I'm sorry I brought it up," I said, "But I didn't like knowing that much about you and not saying anything."

I trailed off when he took my hand and pulled me to him, wrapping his strong arms around my waist as he studied my face with warm, serious eyes.

"You're not like any woman I've dated before," he said. "The women I know would be trying to play me, and you're honest to a fault."

I opened my mouth to say something—I had no idea what, but probably something embarrassing. Holden saved me from myself. His mouth came down on mine, his lips pressing in a gentle kiss before his tongue flicked out, tasting me. My body caught fire. Without thinking, I pressed closer, parting my legs a little, feeling his cock swell behind his jeans.

I reached out my tongue to touch his. The instant we

connected, the kiss exploded. His arms tightened, drawing me hard against him. His mouth was hungry, moving against mine in a kiss so blatantly possessive, so claiming, it would have hurt if it hadn't felt so perfect. Just as I was getting my bearings, Holden lifted me. Instinctively, I wrapped my legs around his hips as he carried me to his kitchen.

"I've been staring at my island all day, wishing I'd done this last night." He set me down on the hard surface and said, "Unbutton your jeans."

At his order and the thrill of his hot, dark eyes on me, a rush of wet heat hit between my legs. Normally, I didn't like being told what to do, but when Holden got bossy with me, I loved it. With shaking hands, I unsnapped my jeans. Sitting on the counter, it was impossible to push them down, but I slowly lowered the zipper, loving the way his eyes flared at the rasp of metal. I hooked my thumbs at the waist and waited. I wasn't disappointed.

"Lay back and slide off your jeans," Holden ordered, his voice rough.

I did as he commanded, the marble deliciously cool against my heated skin. Staring up at the high ceiling of Holden's kitchen, I wiggled my hips and pushed both my jeans and my underwear down. When they were far enough, I let gravity do the work, kicking my feet a few times until the fabric hit the floor in a soft thump. I waited, the tension in my belly winding tighter. He was silent, unmoving, and I started to feel exposed.

"Now your shirt. Take it all off."

In my head, I stripped off my shirt and bra in a sexy, graceful tease. I think reality was more of a rushed fumble, but I didn't care. I wanted to be naked for Holden. I needed whatever was going to come next.

Again, he fell silent, and I waited, feeling my pussy getting wetter, my bare nipples drawing tighter, my entire body readying for him. When I felt a finger land on the inside of my right knee, tracing a line up to my pussy, I knew what to do.

With a moan that was half-anticipation and half-pleasure, I opened my legs. The stroke of his tongue, following the path of his finger, was a decadent torture. He was close, so close, to touching me where I needed him the most. I opened my legs wider, inviting him in. He didn't make me wait. His tongue came down flat on my clit, tasting, pressing, dragging a high-pitched sound from my throat.

I'd never really had a man's mouth there before. Not like this. Not one who knew what he was doing. Holden wasn't going to take another lick and move away, saying it tasted funny, or it was his turn. No, Holden was going to put his mouth between my legs and eat me until I came.

Just the thought of it cranked the tension inside me a notch tighter.

He traced a finger around my wet, slippery core, murmuring, "So sweet. You have the sweetest pussy, Josephine. I have to taste you before I fuck you."

No argument from me. I think I whispered, "Please, Holden," before he sucked my clit into his mouth and drove one finger inside me. His finger didn't stretch me like his cock, but it was enough to make me feel full, so full. His mouth moved on me, sucking, licking, as he added another finger. I squirmed, wanting to thrust against him, wanting his cock, wanting to more.

He teased me, reading my body, understanding my responses better than I did. Again and again, he brought me right to the edge, leaving me gasping and begging, before backing off. He lifted his head from between my legs, only once, to say,

"Play with your nipples, Josephine."

I'd never touched myself in front of a man before, but there was no way I was going to say no to Holden. Lifting a trembling hand from the cool marble, I traced my fingertips around my tight nipples, shivering at the sweet spark of pleasure.

His tongue licked at me, pressing into my swollen clit, giving me just the right pressure. My hips surged up to his mouth and my fingers pinched, my body falling out of my control and under Holden's.

The orgasm tore through me, and my pussy clamped down on Holden's fingers. He fucked me with them harder, sucking at my clit in strong pulls, dragging out the waves of pleasure until I couldn't breathe.

When I came back to myself, Holden was sitting on one of the stools beside the island, cradling me in his arms. I was dazed from coming so hard, and I lifted my face to him, instinctively seeking his touch. I tasted myself on his lips. Any other time, I would have thought it weird, but at that moment, it felt perfect.

"I really did mean to feed you first," he said when he lifted his head from mine.

"I'd rather you fuck me," I said. Not that I hadn't just had the orgasm of a lifetime, but I could feel his hard cock beneath my ass, and I wanted it inside me. I knew he wanted it too.

"If you insist."

Holden carried me to his bedroom, laid me gently on the sheets, and grabbed a condom from his bedside table. He was naked a second later and between my legs, pressing his thick cock inside my swollen pussy a second after that. I'd thought his fingers had filled me, but nothing was like his cock. The stretch was so much, it was almost pain, and I loved it. I clung to his hips with my thighs and moved into him with every thrust, my fingers clamped on his shoulders.

He didn't last long, but I didn't need him to. I was coming again after only a few minutes, gasping his name as I went wild beneath him. He gave into his orgasm, groaning, "Josephine," then collapsed half on top of me, breathing hard. He rolled over, pulling me with him so I was draped over his chest, his fingertips stroking my back in lazy circles.

Eventually, he said, "If we keep fucking like this, we might kill ourselves. Or starve to death."

"Then let's eat dinner before we have sex again," I said. "Just in case."

"Deal."

We lay there a few more minutes, which was a good thing, because I think every muscle in my body was too relaxed to move. I had no idea sex like that even existed, much less had I ever done it multiple times in twenty-four hours. It seemed impossible that exactly a day ago, I was driving Stuart to dinner for our doomed blind date. As awful as that date had been, this date with Holden was winning for the best date in the universe.

Nothing that came after was a letdown. When we finally got up, he cooked an amazing dinner of grilled salmon, asparagus, and apple tarts, though he confessed that it was one of the few dishes he could make and he'd bought the tarts at the bakery down the street. I didn't care. The effort he made called to my heart.

After we ate, we sprawled on his couch to watch a movie, though that lasted fewer than five minutes before I slid to my knees between his legs and sucked his cock. Holden's cock was the first I'd truly wanted in my mouth, and ever since he'd laid me out on the island, I'd been wondering what he would taste like on my tongue. The answer was that he tasted magnificent, salty and male and perfect. I wanted him to come in my mouth, but Holden had other ideas, and before I knew it, he was fucking me again. I didn't complain.

I spent the night, and this time, when I woke, I didn't sneak out. I had a lecture first thing, and I had to get home to change, but I woke Holden before I left. His dark eyes blinked open when I said his name, his arms coming up to pull me on top of him, his sleep-heavy voice whispering, "Josephine." I kissed him longer than I should have before I pulled free.

"I'll call you later," he mumbled into his pillow when I finally went to leave. I leaned down to give him one last kiss on his closed eyelids before racing out the door to class. The weekend had started with a disaster, but it had ended in a dream.

CHAPTER SEVEN

JOSEPHINE

I FLOATED THROUGH MY MONDAY, BUOYED ON A HIGH of fantastic sex and lack of sleep. Other than checking my phone too often, I tried to put Holden out of my mind and concentrate on school. He didn't call or text all day. By dinner, I put my phone away so I'd stop checking, only to miss his call. I called him back and left a voicemail. I knew it was way too soon to expect daily contact, but I missed him. Annoyed that I was so attached after one date, and afraid I was going to morph into a meme of an overly attached girlfriend, I told myself to chill out and focus on my own life.

For the most part, it worked, though every time my mind drifted to Holden, I swear my nipples perked up, and I had to fight the urge to press my legs together. One weekend, not even forty-eight hours, and he had my body trained. Tuesday passed without a call or a text. By Wednesday morning, I had a hollow feeling in my chest and Emily had stopped asking if he'd called. After a rushed lunch, I headed to the Sonification Lab to meet with my group, resolutely not looking at the bench where I'd seen Holden just a few days before. I ran into Darren just inside the doors and walked up to the lab with him, groaning in annoyance when he asked, "How's Prince Charming?"

"Fine," I answered, not planning to go into the sad detail of my love life with Darren. No way he needed to know that I'd slept with Prince Charming the night we'd met and again on our first date, and now, he wasn't calling. It wasn't exactly an original story. I don't know why I'd thought it was going to be different for me.

"I didn't think he'd be your type," Darren said, an odd intensity in his voice. I looked at him, suddenly uncomfortable. He'd asked me out earlier in the year and I'd turned him down. I'd done it gently, but I hadn't thought dating someone on my project was a good idea. Things could get intense, and bringing a personal relationship into it didn't seem smart. That, and I wasn't attracted to him. At all. He was nice enough, but I liked a guy who showered more than twice a week. I know, my standards were too high.

"I don't think I have a type," I said, trying to end the conversation.

"I guess he's every girl's type," Darren went on, as if I hadn't spoken. "Rich."

"I don't care about that," I protested. "And it's not like there's really anything going on. We only went out once."

"Did you see the paper this morning?" he asked, his voice expectant.

"No, why?"

"Let me see if I can find it," he said, taking his phone out of his pocket and tapping on the screen as he went on, "I never look at this crap, but my roommate's girlfriend loves the Style section, and she left it open this morning." He tapped a few more times, then held the phone up in front of me. "Here."

It was a picture of Holden, his arm around a gorgeous, very busty redhead, smiling down at her with clear affection. The date on the article was the day before. The headline said something about the Winters family and a charity event. I bit my lip, forcing back the stab of pain, and shrugged, pretending a nonchalance I didn't feel.

"We only went out once," I said, using every ounce of self-control I had to hide the nausea turning my stomach inside out. I barely heard Darren as he said,

"Well, you know who he is, right? He's got a different girlfriend every week. He and his cousin are huge players. My roommate's girlfriend couldn't shut up about it. I guess she knows someone who dated him and said he's amazing in bed, but an asshole otherwise. You're better off without him."

"I guess," I said, shrugging again. I would have bet everything that Holden wasn't an asshole. Maybe there was another explanation for the picture. I wasn't going to condemn him based on a picture in the paper. That would be foolish. If he called, I'd let him tell me about the redhead.

If he called.

With each hour that passed, Holden calling was looking less and less likely.

I followed Darren to the lab, ignoring him talking about Holden and his cousin, nodding along like I was listening. I didn't have the energy to tell him to shut up. I was afraid that if I opened my mouth to object to everything he was saying, I would start to cry. I was not going to cry in the middle of lab. I could at least wait until I got home and crawled into bed with a sappy movie and some ice cream.

I headed straight for my workstation and went back to poring over the code I'd written, trying to isolate the bug, while Darren and Angie worked on tweaking the glasses. When Darren asked to use my phone for a test, I handed it over, saying only, "Use the newest version of the app. I updated it when I got here."

I wasn't paying too much attention to what they were doing until I heard Angie shout, "You got it! You got it!" Tearing my eyes from the lines of code on my screen, I watched as my phone connected to the glasses with a wire and began to vibrate in a pattern when Angie turned the glasses until they faced an obstacle. I hadn't found the problem with the Bluetooth, and we were nowhere close to working out the patterns for different obstacles, but the spatial field recognition was working.

Mesmerized by the sight of months of work coming to fruition, I almost forgot my recent heartbreak. Almost. Beneath my excitement every time the phone buzzed, that hollow place in my chest echoed at me, reminding me that I'd lost something I didn't even know I wanted.

I stayed later than the rest of the team, ducking their attempts to get me to join them for a drink. We had a lot to celebrate, but I wasn't in the mood. I spent another hour squinting at the screen until my head was pounding before I gave up and dragged myself home. As much as I loved her, I was grateful Emily wouldn't be there. She had her weekly gaming meet with her team, the one night of the week they put aside their projects and played together. I knew she wouldn't be home until well after I was asleep.

My head throbbed each time my feet hit the pavement. By the time I opened my apartment door, all I wanted was to close my eyes. I dropped my phone and bag in the kitchen and headed straight for bed, peeling off my clothes once I shut my door behind me. As soon as I was down to my t-shirt, I crawled between the covers and let my eyes shut, willing myself to sleep.

Sleep didn't come. Instead, now that I was away from curious eyes, the hollow place in my chest expanded to my stomach, leaving me feeling as if all the happiness had been sucked out of me. Stupidly, I didn't care about our triumph in the lab. Alone in my bed, I longed for Holden with an intensity that was absurd, considering how little time we'd spent together.

Funny, you'd think it would be the orgasms that would be on my mind. I'd never had sex like that, and I probably never would again. Holden had known my body better than I did, and he'd made every part of me sing for him.

But I didn't miss the sex. Well, I did, but it wasn't what made hot tears seep from beneath my closed eyelids. No, that came from remembering the way his fingertips had traced over my back as we'd lain together in his bed. The way he smelled, woodsy and male. The way he'd understood my problems at the lab and commiserated without trying to solve them for me. The way, aside from my mentioning his family, we'd fit so well together. He'd managed to push every sexual boundary I had, yet make me completely comfortable otherwise.

When I'd left his bed Monday morning, it had never occurred to me that he would blow me off. I was tempted to think there was some comical misunderstanding going on, but he had my number and knew where I lived. Even if that picture of him with the redhead was a mistake, I'd left him a message two days before and he'd never called back. He didn't have amnesia, and if he'd been in some horrible accident, I would have known. It would have been all over the *Atlanta Journal-Constitution*. I was going to have to face facts. Holden had gotten what he wanted from me. We were over. He wasn't going to call.

As that depressing knowledge sunk in, I began to sob in earnest. Curled up in my quilt, I cried myself to sleep, hoping I'd be able to wash Holden out of my heart with my tears. I had a terrible feeling it wasn't going to be that easy.

CHAPTER EIGHT

HOLDEN

I SAT AT MY DESK IN THE BACK OFFICE AT MANA, scowling at the accounting program on my screen. Neither of us really enjoyed accounting. Normally our club manager handled the books, but he was on vacation and I was in such a foul mood, Tate had banished me from the club.

He may have had a point. I'd been at the bar, waiting for a beer, and had shot down a co-ed so hard, she'd gone back to her friends in tears. Maybe I'd been a little harsh, but her bleached hair had reminded me of the sunlit streaks in Josephine's dirty blonde. Beside the memory of Josephine, the co-ed had looked like a plastic doll in her short, low-cut dress, her fake boobs and fake hair all shouting, "Look at me!"

When she'd put her hand on my crotch and called me by name, I'd told her to get her hands off my cock and go slut it up somewhere else. Not the most gentlemanly response I could have given, I know. The co-ed had burst into loud sobs, running off with an exaggerated flounce that had almost tossed her tits out of her dress. Tate, standing at the other end of the bar, had grabbed my beer from the bartender, shoved it into my hand, and said, "Go back in the office before you scare away any more paying customers."

I was too pissed off to argue. I tried to tell myself I didn't know what was wrong with me, but that was a lie. I knew exactly what was wrong. Fucking Josephine. Or, more accurately, not fucking Josephine. She'd left my bed Monday morning, and that was the last I'd seen of her. Four days with no Josephine. I'd called her Monday night, and she'd called me back, leaving a halting message asking me to call her. That was the last I'd heard from her.

The mess at work that had kept me busy all day Monday had gotten worse by Tuesday. I'd been stuck in conferences until Tuesday night and had gone straight home to pass out. I didn't get clear of it until Wednesday afternoon. Since then, I'd called her five times. Nothing. I'd texted her. Nothing. I knew the crisis at WGC had delayed my call long enough that she would be pissed, but I'd more than made up for it since. I'd left messages asking her to call. Five of them. It was more than clear that she was done with me.

Fuck her. At the thought, I groaned, putting my head down on my desk. I wanted to. I really did. If only it were as simple as a fuck. I didn't need Josephine to get off. The problem was, I wanted her for so much more than that. I remembered the co-ed at the bar and glared at my computer.

Most of the women I met were like her, thinking because my family was rich and prominent, they could lead me around by my dick. The women who pursued my older brothers and cousins were subtler, better at the game. Tate and I got the young ones, the stupid college girls who thought a tight body and a willingness to fuck were all that it took.

Unfortunately for them, Tate and I had earned our reputations. We'd fucked more than our share of greedy girls hoping to latch onto our cocks and win a shot at the easy life. I wasn't interested. I'd seen my oldest brother, Aiden, through an unhappy marriage. Elizabeth was, on the surface, the polar opposite of the blonde at the bar. Aiden's ex-wife was cultured, elegant, and ice-cold. She'd been born to marry a man like Aiden, groomed to run an estate like the one we'd grown up in, taught from birth how to catch a man like my brother. In her heart, she was no better than the girl I'd insulted.

The packaging might be more refined, but Elizabeth was like all the rest, hoping to spend her life enjoying Aiden's wealth while she led him around by his dick.

It could have worked if Aiden had lived a different life. He'd married Elizabeth, I think, under the assumption that she was the kind of woman he was supposed to marry. On the outside, she wasn't much different from my mother. Tate's mom had been a doctor, but my mother had been raised, like Elizabeth, to marry wealth. She was known for her parties, her charity balls, and lunches at the club.

The rest of the world never saw how much she loved her family. She'd loved my father to distraction, and she'd always had time for her children. When my aunt and uncle had died, she'd taken in Gage, Vance, and Tate with open arms, treating them as if they were her own.

My Mom had been pure love, and I think Aiden had hoped that, somehow, Elizabeth had the same inside her. When he'd realized that she didn't, and never would, he'd divorced her.

Aiden wasn't going to settle for less than what our parents had, and neither was I. I'd been bored with easy sex and grasping women for a while. Josephine had seemed like the answer to a prayer. Too bad I wasn't the answer to one of hers.

I'll admit, I was taking her brush-off with little grace and a lot of sulking. I'd always been on the other side, though I never said I'd call when I wasn't going to. But I'd slept with women and then blown them off. It's pretty much all I'd done until Josephine. I couldn't quite believe she was doing it to me.

The door to the office cracked open and Tate stuck his head inside. "Is it safe to come in, or are you going to make me cry?" he asked.

I grunted in response, hoping he'd take that to mean he should leave. It was not my day. He came in and shut the door firmly behind him.

"Are you going to sulk in here all night?" he asked, sitting on the edge of the desk. I didn't answer. "Did you at least get through the receipts?" I continued to ignore him.

"Why don't you just go over to her place and ask her what's up?" he asked in an overly reasonable tone of voice. I glared at him.

"Because I'm not going to beg," I said, hearing the false bravado. I was a mess, and I worried I was precariously close to doing exactly that. "Would you go ask some girl why she hadn't called?" I asked.

"Hell no," Tate said. "But I never give a fuck about the girls I date. Well, not true. A fuck is all I give. I'm more than happy for them to ghost on me. Anyway, I thought Josephine wasn't 'some girl'. I thought she was different."

I shrugged. I knew if I said what I was thinking, that I'd *thought* she was different, that she wasn't just *some girl*, I'd only sound even more pathetic. Briefly, I thought about dumping the accounting, going out to the bar, and getting wasted. Maybe picking up some random girl and fucking her.

The thought left my mind as soon as it entered. I was sulking, but I wasn't an idiot. If there was a chance of working things out with Josephine, I wasn't going to ruin it by fucking someone else, especially when I didn't want another woman. I could still get wasted, but I closed down that idea as well. All that would get me was hung over and more miserable than I already was.

"I have to get through this shit," I said, shuffling through the receipts in front of me and hoping Tate would take the hint. He did, clapping me on the back once before leaving.

"She's just a girl," he said, shutting the door behind him. Narrowing my eyes at the accounting program on my screen, I blocked out thoughts of Josephine and forced myself to get to work.

CHAPTER NINE

JOSEPHINE

"THE DOORBELL IS RINGING," EMILY SHOUTED FROM the kitchen. I was just out of the shower, my hair in a towel, putting lotion on. I knew Em hated to answer the door, but I wasn't in any condition to do it myself.

"You have to get it," I shouted back. She must have answered it, because I didn't hear anything else. Curious, I finished with the lotion, put on my thick terrycloth robe, and pulled a comb through my hair before going to see who was at our door. I knew that for a lot of people, Thursday night was the beginning of the weekend, but not for me. I had a full day of classes the next day and zero desire to go out. I emerged from the bathroom to find Emily standing in front of the door, her arms crossed over her chest, glaring at a man who wasn't Holden but looked almost exactly like him. This must be the cousin. Tate.

"Can I help you?" I asked, trying to think of a reason Holden's cousin would be in my apartment. It was pretty clear Holden wasn't interested in me anymore. Why would he send his cousin over here?

Tate's blue eyes were locked on Emily, an odd, slightly bemused expression on his face. When she snapped her fingers in front of him, I knew he must be making her nervous. Emily was only rude when she was nervous. He gave her a slow smile and caught her snapping fingers in his, turning them so he could kiss the back of her hand. Swoon. Emily's cheeks flared pink, and she snatched back her hand.

"Hello?" I said, not sure I wanted to interrupt whatever was going on between Tate and my so very shy roommate. Tate looked smitten. But Emily was not the girl for him. Em was gorgeous, taller than me, very curvy, with straight, shiny dark hair, and clear gray eyes fringed with lashes so thick, she never needed mascara.

But she didn't date, barely went out, and would have no idea how to handle a man like Tate Winters. If he was anything like Holden, he'd use Emily and toss her away. She didn't need her first experience with a guy to end in a broken heart.

Suddenly worried, I stepped between them, gently pushing Em behind me. Looking up, I met Tate's eyes and asked, "What are you doing here? What do you want?"

Just the sight of him, so much like Holden, was painful. He crossed his arms over his chest and said,

"I told him you wouldn't be worth it. That you'd just end up like all the others. But even I didn't think you'd use him and then blow him off."

He wasn't making any sense. I heard his words, but I couldn't get them to fall in the right order in my head. Me using Holden? What the hell was he talking about?

"She didn't use him," Emily cut in as she stepped out from behind me. She was pissed of, her back stiff, one arm wrapped around herself and the other raised, finger pointing at Tate in stabs of motion as she lectured, "Jo didn't use him. He used *her*! He took her out, swept her off her feet, and then didn't call. That's the definition of blowing someone off."

Tate looked from Emily to me, then back to Emily. He shook his head at her and grabbed her fingers again, holding her hand in his as he said, "Monday and Tuesday weren't his fault. We had a huge blow-up at work and he was stuck putting out fires until Wednesday morning. And he still managed to call your girl."

"Yeah, once. That was it. She never heard from him again," Emily shouted, trying to wrestle her hand back from him, this time unsuccessfully.

I could speak for myself, probably should have, but I was fascinated by the interaction between Emily and Tate. Not that I was letting it go on. She deserved better. But I couldn't remember the last time I saw her go head to head with a stranger. Friends or teammates on a project, sure. But not strangers, especially strange men.

"He's called her three fucking times a day," Tate said, tugging on Em's hand for emphasis. "Left her messages. Now, he looks like someone kicked his fucking puppy, and I'm pissed."

I stared at Tate in shock as he looked at me and demanded, "What is *wrong* with you?"

I didn't say a thing, my head reeling. He had *not* called me three times a day. He'd called me once, and I'd called him back. I may have even texted him—something I hadn't told Emily—and he hadn't responded to that either. Before I could jump in to defend myself, Emily wrenched her hand out of Tate's grip and yelled,

"Nothing is wrong with her. She came back on Monday all moony eyed over your cousin, then he blew her off and went out with some redhead. What's wrong with *him*?"

"He didn't go out with anyone," Tate said, looking at Emily as if she were unhinged.

"Darren showed Jo a picture. I looked it up. Tuesday night, he was out with a redhead while Jo was crying herself to sleep."

"Hey," I said, affronted. They both looked at me, annoyed I'd interrupted. "He doesn't need to hear that part," I directed to Em. She set her jaw and folded her arms, resolute.

"It's the truth," she said. "He should know what a jerk his cousin is."

"Show me the picture," Tate said. "Holden didn't go out with anyone Tuesday night. He was shut up in the office with me, dealing with a crisis."

Emily pulled her phone from her pocket, tapped on the screen for a minute, then shoved it at Tate. He studied the picture for a second before hooting with laughter. He handed her back her phone, pulled out his own, tapped a few times, and showed Emily the screen.

"That picture is a reprint. And here's Holden, with me, his brother Jacob, and his *sister*, Charlie," he said, sounding smug as Em studied his phone with a suspicious gaze. She shoved the phone back at him without a comment. Finally, Tate looked at me.

"He's called you. Seriously, he called multiple times."

Afraid to hope he was telling the truth, I stared a him for almost a full minute before walking to the kitchen table, picking up my phone, and handing it to him.

"Take a look," I said. "I haven't gotten a call since Monday night."

Tate tapped his way through my phone, I'm sure checking the call history and text messages. He finally said, "You could have erased them."

I threw my hands in the air, then grabbed my phone back. "Why would I do that? I'm not the one playing a game here."

"Someone is," Tate said, an ominous tone in his voice. "Because Holden definitely called you. I know his phone works. I used it myself this morning, and he'd know if something was wrong with it."

"I've made calls on mine. Look." I handed the phone back to Tate. "I texted Holden yesterday."

Emily gave me an accusing look. "You didn't tell me that."

I looked away, feeling my cheeks heat. I normally told her everything, but she'd been so pissed at him on my behalf, I hadn't wanted to confess my weakness.

"Sorry," I whispered. "I couldn't stop myself."

Emily, never one to hold a grudge, at least not against me, wrapped her arm around my shoulders and gave me a squeeze, whispering back, "Something is up. I actually believe him."

"I kind of do too," I said, afraid to hope Tate might be telling the truth. I'd missed Holden with a hollow ache that was only getting worse. It was too much to imagine he might be feeling the same way.

Tate finished with my phone and handed it back. "Holden didn't get that text," he said. "I was with him when you sent it. We were in the office, and both of our phones were out. I would have seen it come in."

I stared down at my phone, my mind turning the odd problem over and over, looking for an answer. There was no way the phone had spontaneously decided to malfunction on specific calls. If it were broken, it would be dropping calls randomly. Not one phone number. Pulling up my call history, I double-checked Holden's record and found it wasn't blocked.

I liked solving puzzles. Like a sleepwalker, my brain occupied with the mystery, I headed for my laptop in the living room. I took a cable from the drawer in the coffee table, hooked my phone to my computer, and opened a jailbreak program that would let me get into the operating system of the phone. Everything looked normal. Whatever was wrong was hiding from me.

Following a hunch, I opened a virus program a friend had been working on. Emily, peering over my shoulder, said, "Good call."

The program took a few minutes to run, and the three of us watched its progress on my screen, our breath held as numbers rolled by, a line of green getting longer as the software scanned my phone and found nothing. I started to sit back, defeated, when a red STOP sign popped up and my laptop gave an angry beep.

VIRUS DETECTED

"What the hell?" I asked. I gave the program the order to quarantine the virus so I could take a closer look. When it was done, I opened it up to study the code. A few lines in, and I was seeing red. That bastard. Surging to my feet, I pushed past Emily. I had to get dressed. I had some geek ass to kick.

"What?" Emily asked, following me down the hall. "What did you find?"

"That was Darren's virus," I said, searching through my drawers for clothes. I dragged on my jeans, pulled a sweatshirt over my head, and shoved flip flops on my feet.

"Are you sure?" she asked.

"Positive. He has signatures all over his code. I gave him a hard time about it and told him it was sloppy and he'd better never make a virus, or he'd get caught in a second. He's too smart to be so dumb."

"What an asshole," she said, turning to Tate, who had waited for us at the end of the hall. She said, "Darren is the one who showed her that picture of Holden with his sister. He has a crush on Jo, and she turned him down."

"I'm going to kill that little shit," I said.

Tate stepped in front of me as I stormed to the door of my apartment. "Where do you think you're going?" he asked, looking like he was stifling a laugh.

"Get out of my way," I said, stepping to the side. Tate mirrored me, clearly not willing to let me leave until I answered his question. "I'm going to Darren's to kick his ass."

"No, you're not," he said. "Holden would kill me if I let anything happen to you. Let me call him."

"No," I said. "This whole thing is my fault. I *gave* Darren my phone. I never thought he'd do something like this. He made me miserable for days. He *knew* I was miserable. I thought he was my friend."

I stepped to the side again, trying to get around Tate. He easily blocked me. "Holden will understand," he said. "Let's go to the club, and you can explain."

"Sure," I said, my vision going red as I thought about what Darren had done. "After I talk to Darren."

"I'm driving," Tate said, taking my arm in his hand.

"What?" Emily and I asked in unison.

"Do you think I'm going to let you confront this guy on your own? If you won't talk to Holden first, I'm at least going to watch your back."

"I'm coming too," Emily said from behind me. I looked at her in shock. Jumping into the middle of a drama was not

Emily's style. "Well, I'm not letting you go off with him." She pointed at Tate like he was a serial killer holding me at knifepoint.

"Fine," I said.

I didn't care. I just wanted to get moving. Darren wasn't my best friend, but we'd known each other for two years. I wouldn't fully believe he could have done something like this until he admitted it to my face.

CHAPTER TEN

JOSEPHINE

TATE DROVE US TO DARREN'S APARTMENT, ME IN THE front seat and Emily in the back, leaning forward so she was more between us than behind.

"I heard you're working on a new physics engine. And that you've written advancements in emergent gaming into Syndrome 2," she said, the pulse thudding in the side of her neck. I'd expected Em to disappear into the backseat once her anger at Tate had drained away. I should have known her curiosity about their company would prod her to speak despite her shyness.

Tate didn't respond, but I saw his lips twitch in a half-smile from the corner of my eye. He was messing with her. My head wrapped up in the problems with Darren and thoughts of Holden, I wasn't sure how I felt about that. Maybe it was good for Emily to step out of her comfort zone.

"Well?" she demanded. "Is it true?"

"Is what true?" Tate asked evenly. I stifled a laugh when Em gritted her teeth.

"Either! Both! It seems unlikely that you could be doing both, but I know you have a huge team at WGC and they're crazy talented, so it's possible, but . . ."

She trailed off as it became clear Tate wasn't going to answer her. I could have sworn I heard a low growl in her throat. I'd always known gaming and computers were the key to getting past Emily's shell, but I couldn't quite believe how open she was being with Tate. Normally, a guy like him—gorgeous, rich, successful, and a player—would have frozen her mouth shut. Instead, she was almost sparring with him. Still, what happened next took me by surprise.

Tate pulled the car into a spot on the street a block from Darren's apartment and turned in his seat to face Emily. "Go out to dinner with me," he ordered.

"What?" she asked, her voice more like a squeak.

"Go out to dinner with me, and I'll bring you to WGC

for dessert. I might even let you see a demo of what we're working on."

Emily's eyes flashed wide, excitement flaring through the clear gray for just a moment before a wall came crashing down. She looked away from Tate, drew in a short breath, and said, "No, thank you," in a cool, prim tone.

It was Tate's turn for the wide eyes. Looking at the blank expression on his face, I wondered if Emily was the first girl to turn him down. Taking in his thick, dark hair, perfect cheekbones and full lips, I wouldn't have been surprised to find out that no female had ever said no to him.

Part of me wanted to referee whatever was going on between my best friend and Holden's cousin, but I had an ass to kick before I could see Holden. Tate and Emily could work out their issues later.

I opened the door of the car, shaking them out of their absorption. Tate followed me out of the car, Emily just behind. I strode to the door of the building, then stopped so abruptly, Tate had to put a hand on my shoulder to keep from walking into me. Turning to him, I asked in a small voice,

"He really called? You're not screwing with me?"

Tate leaned down and met my eyes with his. We'd only just met, and though he looked like Holden, his dark blue eyes were all his own. Still, they seemed sincere when he squeezed my shoulder and said, "He's a mess. I swear, he's called you at least three times a day. I'm not setting you up to get burned. That's on your friend upstairs. Let's go take care of him so you can put my boy out of his misery."

I nodded, reassured. I'd accepted Holden walking away so easily because it made sense. In my world, billionaire hot guys didn't fall for geeky chicks who looked more like they belonged in a library than on a runway. It had been too easy to believe he'd slept with me and then forgotten my name. Believing that he was missing me as much as I missed him? That was a lot harder.

With Tate's reassurance to bolster me, I opened the door and climbed the stairs to the second floor. I'd only been to Darren's apartment a few times, but I remembered how to get there. My anger had me on auto-pilot.

I pounded on the cheap wooden door without pause until it swung open beneath my hand. Darren's face broke into a smile at the sight of me. His expression dimmed when he saw Tate and Emily behind me. Shifting uncomfortably, he shoved his hands in his back pockets and said, "Hey, Jo, what's up?"

I held up my phone and waved in in his face. "Leave something in my phone, Darren?"

His eyes flicked from me to Tate to Emily, landing on

my phone. He made a grab for it, but I tucked it in my back pocket. When he looked as if he'd go for it anyway, Tate stepped closer.

"Don't even think about it," he said, his arms crossed, his body slightly angled between me and Darren. He wasn't getting in my way, but it was obvious he'd take Darren down if he tried to lay a finger on me.

Darren slid his hands back into his pockets and tried for an innocent expression. "I don't know what you're talking about, Jo. I haven't touched your phone."

"You're an idiot, Darren," I said. "I don't know how someone so smart can be such a stupid tool. Everyone saw you working on my phone on Wednesday. I have a copy of the virus, and it's got your signatures all over it. What the hell were you thinking?"

He shrugged, not meeting my eyes. "You were just supposed to think he was blowing you off. He's already stopped calling. I was going to take it off tomorrow in the lab. You never would have known I did anything."

Tears sprang to my eyes as I realized he was right. If Tate hadn't confronted me, I would have just assumed Holden was done with me. Darren would have erased the virus, and I never would have known what he'd done. My chance with Holden would have gone up in smoke, a victim of Darren's jealousy.

"Why?" I asked, willing myself not to cry in front of him. "I thought we were friends."

"We are," he protested. "You're too good for that guy. He's fucked half the city. He's an entitled man-whore. You can do so much better than him—"

Darren didn't get to finish his tirade against Holden. Before I could think it through, my fist shot out, and I hit him on the face. Once. Then twice. Pain exploded in my hand, but I hit him again a third time, hard enough that he stumbled back, tripping over his own feet and landing on the floor.

"Don't talk about Holden like that," I said, my temper so lost I wondered if I'd ever find it. "You know nothing about him. He's a good man. He deserves everything. He deserves so much better than an asshole like you fucking with his life."

I took a step forward, maybe to kick him, I don't know. I wasn't thinking clearly. A strong arm hooked around my waist, pulling me back into a hard chest. Tate swung me around until I was facing Emily.

"I think you're done, hot shot," he said. "His nose is bleeding, and so is your hand."

I checked my hand, suddenly feeling the throb in my now bloody knuckles. I did *not* know how to throw a punch. As the adrenaline faded, my hand started to seriously hurt.

"Fine," I said to Tate. To Darren, still on the floor, I said, "I'm turning you in. I have the virus, and anyone who's worked with you will be able to verify it's yours. Plus, you just confessed in front of witnesses, genius. You're fucked. Have a nice life."

Cradling my hand against my chest, I turned for the stairwell at the end of the hall. I was done wasting time on Darren. All I really wanted was to set things straight with Holden.

CHAPTER ELEVEN

JOSEPHINE

*I*T WAS A SHORT, QUIET RIDE FROM DARREN'S APARTMENT
to Mana. Tate said Holden was there, apparently shut up in
the back office with paperwork. Emily hadn't said a thing
since Tate had asked her out. Tate was equally silent, saying
only that we needed to get ice for my hand before turning
his attention to the road, sneaking looks at Emily in the
rearview, a puzzled expression on his face.

We pulled to a stop in front of Mana, where Tate handed
his keys to a valet and ushered us around the corner to the
same VIP entrance I'd used with Stuart the weekend before.

Tate exchanged a greeting with the bouncer, slapping him on the shoulder as he passed through the open door. Emily followed, ignoring Tate and the bouncer, her head down, body braced against the crowd and music inside. A nightclub wasn't Emily's idea of fun—tons of people, loud music, flashing lights. There was no way she wanted to be here. She was a great friend, but this was above and beyond. I caught up to her and said, "You don't have to come in if you don't want to."

"I'm okay," she said, her voice shaking a little. "I want to see what happens." She shot a grin at me, and I dropped it. If Em was stretching her boundaries, who was I to discourage her?

Tate led us down a back hall, past the restrooms, to a locked door. Pulling a key from his pocket, he opened the door, shoved me through, and locked it behind me.

I was in a cramped office lined with shelves, stacked with papers and boxes. Holden sat hunched over a laptop, scowling at the screen. His dark hair fell in his eyes as if he'd run his fingers through it one too many times. He tapped one finger on the desk in impatience or irritation—I couldn't tell which. I drank in the sight of him. It had been four days since I'd seen him, and it felt like a year. Without looking up from the screen, he said, "What? I'm almost done. Stop bugging me."

I had no idea what to say. *I'm sorry? Darren's an asshole?* Instead, I just stood there, staring at him, before I finally said, "Holden." Just his name. I couldn't manage anything else. His head rose, slowly, and he blinked.

"Holden," I said again, taking a step closer. He stared at me, his dark eyes locked on my face, his expression closed. I pulled my phone out of my pocket with my left hand—my right was throbbing—and held it out to him, saying, "Darren put a virus on it. It stopped me from getting your calls, or you from getting mine. I texted you. I thought you were blowing me off."

I shrugged helplessly as he took the phone from me, turning it over in his hands, as if looking for evidence of the hack when both of us could see that the phone looked completely normal.

"I called you," he said, placing the phone carefully on his desk and standing to face me.

"I know," I said. "Tate told me."

"Tate?" Holden asked. As if he were waiting for his entrance, the key scraped in the lock and the door swung open to reveal Tate, with Emily behind him. Tate handed me a plastic bag filled with ice and looked between us before he said to me, "You good?"

Holden answered for me. "She's good. You can go."

"Jo?" Emily asked, her eyebrows raised.

"I'm good," I said in reassurance, even though I had no idea if I really was. Holden hadn't said much. He definitely hadn't rushed to my side and kissed me senseless, vowing his eternal love for me. Shutting the door behind Tate and Emily, he flipped the deadbolt and watched me press the ice to my hand.

"What happened?" he asked, taking my injured hand in his and smoothing the ice bag gently across my battered fingers. The heat of his hand cradling mine made me a little dizzy. I'd missed touching him. He leaned into me, rubbing his thumb along the side of my pinky finger. "How did you hurt yourself?"

"I punched Darren."

"You what?" He asked, his fingers squeezing mine. I winced, and he loosened his grip, his eyebrows knitting together. "Sorry. Did you say you punched him?"

"He was being an asshole. He was trying to justify what he did, and I . . ." I trailed off and shrugged, embarrassed that I'd hauled off and punched someone. Even if he *was* being an asshole.

"Don't do that again," Holden said. He lifted the ice bag and studied my red, raw knuckles. At least they'd stopped bleeding. "You can really hurt your hand hitting someone if you don't know what you're doing. How many times did you hit him?"

"Three," I said. "But I think I caught his teeth. It hurts."

"It looks like it." He tucked my hand between us and pulled me closer. I leaned into his hard chest and inhaled his woodsy, male scent. My head was spinning from being so close to him. I rested my forehead against Holden and said,

"I thought you were done with me. You didn't call, and then Darren showed me a picture of you with a woman. I didn't know she was your sister."

"I don't think I'm ever going to be done with you, Josephine," Holden said in a low voice. I leaned back to look up into his warm brown eyes.

"I think I'm falling in love with you, Holden Winters," I said. "It's crazy, because I've only known you a week. So maybe it's just the amazing sex."

"It's definitely the sex. But I think I'm falling in love with you too, Josephine Miller. I don't care if it's only been a week. I know what I feel. When I thought you didn't want to see me—"

I placed a finger over his lips. I knew exactly how that had felt. He didn't need to tell me. And I was finished with talking. Sliding my hand around to grip the nape of his neck, I ran my fingers through his thick, silky hair and tugged.

Holden didn't need any more hints. Dipping his head, he brought his lips to mine, brushing over them in a slow, sweet kiss before urging my mouth open and sliding his tongue against mine. I dropped the ice bag on the floor and leaned into Holden, falling into his kiss.

It started sweet, but once I got the taste of him, my knees went weak, my pussy was wet, and the kiss turned hard and hungry. Holden backed me up to his desk, reaching behind me to shove a pile of papers to the side. They fell in a rustling cascade, spilling around our feet. Holden's hands slid beneath my sweatshirt. He gave a low hum when they encountered nothing but bare skin.

"No bra?" He murmured, dragging the fabric over my head.

"I was in a rush. I missed you."

My hands went to the fly of his jeans, my fingers fumbling on the snap, desperate to get to him, needing to feel him inside me again. He had no such problems, flicking open my jeans and peeling them down my legs so fast, it felt like magic. He went to his knees, one arm around my waist as he helped me lift my feet free. I stood above him, naked in his office, grateful he'd thought to lock the door with the deadbolt.

Holden looked up at me, catching my eyes with his. Leaning in, he hovered before my hips, his breath skating over my skin. Shivers ran down my spine at having him so close, at the sheer sexual intent in his eyes. Without looking, he opened the desk drawer and pulled out a condom.

He had condoms in his desk? Reading my mind, Holden shook his head, negating the thought before it could fully form.

"I share the office with Tate. But he won't mind me borrowing one," he said, his words sending puffs of air against my clit. I trembled. Maybe it was the arousal talking, but I said, "I don't care. I trust you, Holden."

I did trust him. I knew, in my soul, that I could trust Holden with my body and my heart. With my everything.

"I won't let you down, Josephine."

I opened my mouth to tell him I wouldn't let him down either, but all that escaped was a strangled squeak as the flat of his tongue came down on my clit. He pressed hard, then licked up, lifting my clit, tugging it, sending sparks of pleasure shooting up my spine. My legs shaking, I reached behind me to brace my hands on the desk, wincing at the pressure on my bruised knuckles.

A little pain didn't matter. I let my legs fall apart, opening for Holden's mouth, moaning aloud as he sucked my clit, his fingers sinking into my hips, holding me still as I squirmed.

"Holden," I cried out, tugging on his hair. As much as I loved his mouth between my legs, I wanted him inside me, fucking me, filling me up. I wanted to kiss him while he took me. I needed to feel so close to him, nothing could ever pull us apart again.

He rose to his feet, and I sat back on the desk, spreading my legs wider, watching with hungry eyes as he lowered his zipper and pushed his jeans down, freeing his thick cock. I'd never seen a cock like Holden's before. Not that I had a ton of experience, but his was thick and long, better than any I'd dreamed of in my hottest fantasies. My mouth watered at the thought of tasting him. Later.

I reached out with my legs and wrapped them around his hips, drawing him closer. He resisted, rolling on the condom. A heart beat later, he was on me, his hands everywhere, his cock pressing into my pussy, stretching me open, filling me up. I cried out with the sheer bliss of it, gripping him with my legs, my arms wrapped around him.

Holden's mouth came down on mine, kissing me with a desperate need as he fucked me hard. The desk rocked back, papers falling to the carpet, then something heavier, cracking to pieces. Holden didn't even slow down, driving me closer and closer to orgasm, kissing me and fucking me with everything he had. I held him tight, moving with him, my pussy clenching around him in hard pulses as he fucked me into heaven.

Holden followed me into release, burying himself to the hilt and freezing there, his arms steel bars around me, holding me to his chest. When his breathing evened out, he said,

"I don't think I'm falling in love with you, Josephine. I know I am."

I let out a shaky laugh, still reeling from the orgasm, my heart tight in my chest. I reached up to press a kiss to the hard line of his jaw, drawing a deep breath, filling my lungs with the potent scent of Holden and sex. Of us. Together. It was primal. Life itself. I had no hesitation when I said,

"I know it too. I love you, Holden."

We stayed there, wrapped in each other, until Holden helped me off the desk and into my clothes. I'd never been into the risk of being discovered. I still wasn't. There was no way I would have had half as much fun if Holden hadn't locked the door. But we were definitely having sex on his desk again. Looking down, I saw his laptop in pieces on the floor.

"Oops," I said. Holden followed my gaze.

"I backed it up," he said. "Right now, I couldn't care less."

He wrapped his arm around me, leading me down the hall, out the VIP door, and down the alley to a private parking area. I saw a sign for Tate, nailed to the wall above an empty parking place.

"Do you think Tate took Emily home?"

"I'm sure he did," Holden said. "He wouldn't have let her walk at this time of night."

"He asked her out, and she said no."

Holden burst out laughing. "It's probably the first time that's ever happened," he said.

"That's what I thought. He looked a little shocked," I said.

Holden started the car and turned down a side alley I hadn't seen, neatly popping out into the street around the corner from the club. He headed for his place, still laughing.

"I should call her," I said, mostly to myself.

"I think we left your phone in my office. The last I saw, it was on my desk."

"Oh." I hoped it wasn't in the same condition as his laptop. "Then I guess we'll have to find out what happened later," I said.

Holden took my hand in his, lacing his fingers through mine. "Later," he agreed. "I'm sure Tate got her home all right. We don't have to call. I went without you for almost four days. I have a lot to make up for."

That was fine with me. "Did you get your problems at work fixed?" I asked.

Holden glanced at me and said, "I did. Why?"

"I was thinking about bailing on my classes tomorrow. Maybe staying in bed all day," I said, keeping my face neutral, my voice even.

"Were you?" Holden asked, playing along. "I think a long weekend sounds like exactly what I need. As long as it involves you, naked. Bed optional."

"I can do that," I said, grinning at him, my heart swelling in my chest, the surge of joy at the love in his eyes almost too much to take. "As long as I'm with you, I have everything I need."

Holden parked the car, and I followed him to the elevator that would take us to his penthouse. Tomorrow was Friday. Barring any unforeseen crises, we had a three-day weekend stretching ahead of us, just Holden and me. Naked. I squeezed my legs together, feeling heat flood my pussy. We'd just had sex. How could I want him this much again? I remembered him unsnapping his jeans in his office and my plan to get my mouth on his beautiful cock.

Licking my lips, I glanced at the front of his jeans as the elevator carried us up to his floor. The second we cleared his door, I was going to strip him naked and have my way with him. Somehow, I didn't think Holden would mind.

The elevator doors slid open, and I stepped through, Holden's hand clasped in mine, ready for whatever was coming next.

Do you want to read Tate and Emily's story?
Keep reading for a sneak peek of The Billionaire's
Secret Love

THE BILLIONAIRE'S SECRET LOVE

TATE

GO OUT TO DINNER WITH ME.

No, thank you.

The conversation echoed in my head. *No, thank you?* Had she really turned me down? I couldn't remember the last time a woman turned me down. For anything. My first reaction was to ignore her and pretend I didn't care.

I couldn't do it.

I had no idea what it was about this girl that had so captured my attention. I'd only met her an hour ago, but I wanted her. I'd gone over to her apartment, geared up to confront her roommate over dumping my cousin, when Emily had opened the door and I'd tumbled head over heels after one look. It was the oldest cliche and one I'd never believed. Until now.

Taken part by part, she wasn't anything special. She shouldn't have been. Medium height, a little on the tall side but not quite tall. Long, straight, dark brown hair. Creamy skin. Gray eyes. And very, very curvy. Her faded jeans fit her sweet, full ass to perfection, and her sweater hung loose off one shoulder, clinging to her round tits. Her clothes hadn't been chosen to show off her body, but they were too well cut to hide it.

Still, it was her eyes that got me. A clear, pure gray, like a lake in winter. She'd swung the door open, and I'd fallen in to those fathomless gray eyes. If I was being honest, I still hadn't pulled myself out.

Thank You

Thanks for reading The Billionaire's Secret Heart!
I hope you enjoyed it!

Don't Miss Out on New Releases, Free Stories and More!!
Join Ivy's Readers Group!
Ivylayne.com/readers-group

Visit me on:
Facebook.com/AuthorIvyLayne
www.IvyLayne.com

Also by Ivy Layne

Don't Miss Out on New Releases, Free Stories and More!!
Join Ivy's Readers Group! Ivylayne.com/readers-group

The Billionaire's Secret - Novella Duology
The Billionaire's Secret Heart
The Billionaire's Secret Love

Scandals of the Bad Boy Billionaires
The Billionaire's Pet
The Billionaire's Promise

About the Author

Ivy Layne has had her nose stuck in a book since she first learned to decipher the English language. Sometime in her early teens, she stumbled across her first Romance, and the die was cast. Though she pretended to pay attention to her creative writing professors, she dreamed of writing steamy romance instead of literary fiction. These days, she's neck deep in alpha heroes and the smart, sexy women who love them.

Married to her very own alpha hero (who rubs her back after a long day of typing, but also leaves his socks on the floor). Ivy lives in the mountains of North Carolina where she and her other half are having a blast raising two energetic little boys. Aside from her family, Ivy's greatest loves are coffee and chocolate, preferably together.

Printed in Great Britain
by Amazon